The Dead, the Dying and the Damned

Cotton Harding, former Civil War soldier and current gunslinger, has no part in the war that is taking place between a brutal Mexican bandit king and the towns he is terrorizing. Harding hates men like Benitez, who kills to live and lives to kill. Harding has come to Mexico to earn money doing what the war had made him good at – killing – and hasn't intended being away for so long.

Harding has found love back in New Mexico, and that love has made him more of a man . . . a man who would stand against a bandit army to save not only the town but his legacy for his love.

In order to stand against that army, he aims to recruit more men like him – good men; at least, good at one thing – killing. Yet in some ways these men are as bad as Benitez. All in all, these men, and Harding himself, are all either dead, dying or damned.

The Dead, the Dying and the Damned

Matt Cole

A Black Horse Western

ROBERT HALE

© Matt Cole 2017
First published in Great Britain 2017
This impression 2018

ISBN 978-0-7198-2471-5

The Crowood Press
The Stable Block
Crowood Lane
Ramsbury
Marlborough
Wiltshire SN8 2HR

www.bhwesterns.com

Robert Hale is an imprint
of The Crowood Press

Typeset by
Derek Doyle & Associates, Shaw Heath
Printed and bound in Great Britain by
4edge Limited, Hockley, Essex

Do good and don't worry to whom.

Mexican Proverb

They tried to bury us; they didn't know we were seeds.

Mexican Proverb

There is no bad that comes without a good.

Mexican Proverb

We all know what we are, but know not what we may be.

Hamlet, Shakespeare

Make Me No Grave

Make me no grave within that quiet place
Where friends shall sadly view the grassy
   mound,
Politely solemn for a little space,
As though the spirit slept beneath the ground.

For me no sorrow, nor the hopeless tear;
No chant, no prayer, no tender eulogy:
I may be laughing with the gods – while here
You weep alone. Then make no grave for me

But lay me where the pines, austere and tall,
Sing in the wind that sweeps across the West:
Where night, imperious, sets her coronal
Of silver stars upon the mountain crest.

Where dawn, rejoicing, rises from the deep,
And Life, rejoicing, rises with the dawn:
Mark not the spot upon the sunny steep,
For with the morning light I shall be gone.

Far trails await me; valleys vast and still,
Vistas undreamed of, canyon-guarded streams,

Lowland and range, fair meadow, flower-girt
   hill,
Forests enchanted, filled with magic dreams.

And I shall find brave comrades on the way:
None shall be lonely in adventuring,
For each a chosen task to round the day,
New glories to amaze, new songs to sing.

Loud swells the wind along the mountain-side,
High burns the sun, unfettered swings the sea,
Clear gleam the trails whereon the vanished
   ride,
Life calls to life: then make no grave for me!

Henry Herbert Knibbs, from *Songs of the Trail*, 1920

PROLOGUE

DEATH AND BEAUTY RIDE TOGETHER

Cotton Harding was riding just below the summit of the ridge of the Basin and Range Region that covered about a third of New Mexico and was to the south of the Rocky Mountain Region. This region extended south from around Santa Fe to Mexico and west to Arizona. This area was marked by rugged mountain ranges, such as the Guadalupe, Mogollon, Organ, Sacramento and San Andres mountain ranges, separated by desert basins. The Rio Grande River flowed north to south through the Basin and Range Region and exited New Mexico in the south to form the border between Texas and Mexico.

He occasionally uplifted his head so as to gaze across the crest, shading his eyes with one hand to thus better concentrate his vision. Both horse and

8

rider plainly exhibited signs of weariness, but every movement of the latter showed ceaseless vigilance, his glance roaming the barren ridges and his left hand taut on the rein. Yet the horse he bestrode scarcely required restraint, advancing slowly, with head hanging low, and only occasionally breaking into a brief trot under the impetus of the spur.

The rider was a man approaching his late thirties, somewhat slender and long of limb, but possessing broad, squared shoulders above a deep chest, sitting the saddle easily in plainsman fashion, yet with an erectness of carriage that suggested military training. The face under the wide brim of the weather-worn slouch hat was clean-shaven, browned by sun and wind and strongly marked, the chin slightly prominent, the mouth firm, the grey eyes full of character and daring. His dress was that of rough service – plain leather 'chaps', showing marks of hard usage, a grey woollen shirt turned low at the neck, with a kerchief knotted loosely about the sinewy bronzed throat. On one hip dangled the holster of a .45 and on the other hung a canvas-covered canteen. His was a figure and face to be noted anywhere, a man from whom you would expect both thought and action, and one who seemed to exactly fit into his wild environment.

Where he rode the very western extreme of the prairie country billowed like the sea, and from off the crest of its higher ridges, the wide level sweep of the plains was visible, extending like a vast brown ocean to the foothills of the far-away mountains.

New Mexico was roughly bisected by the Rio Grande, and the State was marked by broken mesas, wide deserts, heavily forested mountain wildernesses and high, bare peaks. The mountain ranges, part of the Rocky Mountains, rising to their greatest height in the Sangre de Cristo Mountains, were in broken groups, running north to south through central New Mexico and flanking the Rio Grande. In the southwest was the Gila Wilderness. Broad, semi-arid plains, particularly prominent in South New Mexico, were covered with cactus, yucca, creosote bush, sagebrush and desert grasses. Water was rare in these regions, and the scanty rainfall subject to rapid evaporation. The country hardened people.

Some, like Harding, were already hardened by war and killing.

Yet the actual commencement of that drear, barren expanse was fully ten miles distant, while all about where he rode the conformation was irregular, comprising narrow valleys and swelling mounds, with here and there a sharp ravine, riven from the rock, and invisible until one drew up startled at its very brink. The general trend of depression was undoubtedly southward, leading further in the country of Mexico, yet irregular ridges occasionally cut across, adding to the confusion. The entire surrounding landscape presented the same aspect, with no special object upon which the eye could rest for guidance – no tree, no upheaval of rock, no peculiarity of summit, no snake-like trail – all about extended the same dull, dead monotony of brown, sun-baked hills, with slightly greener depressions lying between, interspersed by patches of sand or the white gleam of alkali. It was a dreary, deserted land, parched under the hot summer sun, brightened by no vegetation, excepting sparse bunches of buffalo grass or an occasional stunted sage bush, and disclosing nowhere the slightest sign of human habitation.

The rising sun reddened the crest of the hills, and the rider, halting his willing horse, sat motionless, gazing steadily into the southwest. Apparently, he perceived nothing there unusual, for he slowly turned his body about in the saddle, sweeping his eyes, inch by inch, along the line of the horizon, until the entire circuit had been completed. Then his compressed lips smiled slightly, his hand unconsciously patting the horse's neck.

'I reckon we're still alone, old girl,' he said quietly; the bit of Southern drawl in the voice was beginning to disappear. 'We'll make the town shortly, and take it easy.'

He swung stiffly out of the saddle and, with reins dangling over his shoulder, began the slower advance on foot, the exhausted horse trailing behind. His was not a situation in which he could feel certain of safety, for any ridge might conceal the wary foe, men that usually he would seek to avoid, yet he proceeded now with renewed confidence.

The place was the very heart of the Mexican bandit territory, with every mile either restless or openly on the war-path. Rumours of atrocities from the bandits were being retold the length and breadth of the border, and every report drifting in to either fort or settlement only added to the alarm. Opposing them were the scattered and unorganized settlers lining the more eastern streams, guarded by small detachments of regular troops posted here and there amid that broad wilderness, scarcely within touch of each other.

Everywhere beyond these lines of patrol wandered roaming war parties, attacking travellers on the trails, raiding exposed settlements, and occasionally venturing to try open battle with the small squads of armed men. In this stress of sudden emergency, with every available soldier on active duty, civilians had been pressed into service, and hastily dispatched to warn exposed settlers, guide wagon trains, or carry dispatches between outposts. And thus, our rider, who knew every foot of the plains in this area of the west, merely because he chanced to be discovered unemployed by the harassed commander of a cantonment just without the environs of the New Mexican prairie. Twenty minutes later he was riding swiftly into the southwest. To Harding, this had been merely another page in a career of adventure; for him to take his life in his hands had long ago become an old story. He had quietly performed the special duty allotted him, watched a squadron of troopers trot forth down the valley of the Republican, received the hasty thanks of the peppery little general, and then, having nothing better to do, traded his horse in at the government corral for a fresh mount and started back again for Mexico. For

the greater portion of two nights and a day he had
been in the saddle, but he was accustomed to this, for
he had driven more than one bunch of longhorns up
the Texas trail; hired his guns out to the highest
bidder on several occasions, and as he had slept
three hours overnight, and as his nerves were like
steel, the thought of danger gave him slight concern.
He was thoroughly tired, and it rested him to get out
of the saddle, while the freshness of the morning air
was a tonic, the very breath of which made him for-
getful of fatigue.

After all, this was indeed the very sort of experience which appealed to him, and always had – this
life of peril in the open, under the stars and the sky.
He had constantly experienced it for so long now,
eight years, as to make it seem merely natural. While
he ploughed steadily forward through the shifting
sand of the coulee, his thoughts drifted idly back
over those years, and sometimes he smiled, and occasionally frowned, as various incidents returned to
memory. It had been a rough life, yet one not
unusual to those of his generation.

The Civil War came; he had been born in the
South, and he became a sergeant in a cavalry regi-
ment commanded by a one-time neighbour of his.
He had enjoyed that life and won his spurs, yet it had
cost. There was much not over-pleasant to remember, and those strenuous years of almost ceaseless
fighting, of long night marches, of swift, merciless
raiding, of lonely scouting within the enemy's lines,
of severe wounds, hardship and suffering, had left

their marks on both body and soul. His father had fallen on the field at Antietam, and left him utterly alone in the world, but he had fought on grimly to the end, until the last flag of the Confederacy had been furled. By that time, upon the collar of his tattered grey jacket appeared the tarnished insignia of a captain. The quick tears dimmed his eyes even now as he recalled anew that final parting following Appomattox, the battle-worn faces of his men, and his own painful journey homeward, defeated, wounded and penniless. It was no home when he got there, only a heap of ashes and a few weed-grown acres. No familiar face greeted him; not even a slave was left.

He had honestly endeavoured to remain there, to face the future and work it out alone; he persuaded himself to feel that this was his paramount duty to the State, to the memory of the dead. But those very years of army life made such a task impossible; the dull, dead monotony of routine, the loneliness, the slowness of results, became intolerable. As it came to thousands of his comrades, the call of the West came to him, and at last he yielded, and drifted toward the frontier. The life there fascinated him, drawing him deeper and deeper into its swirling vortex. He became freighter, mail carrier, hunter, government scout, cowboy foreman and a gunfighter.

Once he had drifted into the mountains, and took a chance in the mines, but the wide plains called him back once more to their desert loneliness. What an utter waste it all seemed, now that he looked back upon it. Eight years of fighting, hardship, and rough living, and what had they brought him? The reputation of a hard rider, a daring player at cards, a quick shot, a scorner of danger, and a bad man to fool with – that was the whole of a record barely won. The man's eyes hardened, his lips set firmly, as this truth came crushing home. A pretty life story surely, one to be proud of, and with probably no better ending than an Indian bullet, or the flash of a revolver in some barroom fight.

The narrow valley along which he was travelling suddenly changed its direction, compelling him to climb the rise of the ridge. Slightly below the summit he halted. In front extended the wide expanse of the Arkansas valley, a scene of splendour under the golden rays of the sun, with vivid contrast of colours, the grey of rocks, the yellow of sand, the brown of distant hills, the green of vegetation, and the silver sheen of the stream half hidden behind the fringe of cottonwoods lining its banks. This was a sight Harding had often looked upon, but always with appreciation, and for the moment his eyes swept across from bluff to bluff without thought except for its wild beauty. Then he perceived something which instantly startled him into attention – yonder, close beside the river, just beyond that ragged bunch of cottonwoods, slender spirals of blue smoke were visible. That would hardly be a camp of freighters at this hour of the day, and besides, the Santa Fe trail along here ran close in against the bluff, coming down to the river at the ford two miles further west.

15

No party of plainsmen would ever venture to build a fire in so exposed a spot, and no small company would take the chances of the trail. But surely that appeared to be the flap of a canvas wagon top a little to the right of the smoke, yet all was so far away he could not be certain. He stared in that direction a long while, shading his eyes with both hands, unable to decide. There were three or four moving black dots higher up the river, but so far away he could not distinguish whether men or animals. Only as out-lined against the yellow sand dunes could he tell they were advancing westward toward the ford.

As he tried to put the years of war and killing behind him, though that was how he had made his reputation and earned his money, a face haunted Harding – a woman's face. It was as day like the white-hot ember of a dying campfire; it hung in the shadows that hovered over the unsteady light; it drifted in the shadows beyond.

This hour, when the day had closed and the lonely desert night set in with its dead silence, was one in which Cameron's mind was thronged with memories of a time long past – of a home back in Kettle Springs, of a woman he had wronged and lost, and loved too late . . . perhaps. He certainly hoped it was not too late.

Did she even know the man she loved?

And the more important question was would she be alive once he got to Hermanas Pozos, where she had come in search of him, leaving the safety of their home back in Kettle Springs, New Mexico.

16

CHAPTER 1

THE DYING GIRL

He had always found the surface of the country beautiful, but not as beautiful as Nina Marie Romero. He had travelled over the plains and mesas, ridden the trails through the San Andres, Organ and Franklin mountains running north and south, and at some distance from the boundary between the New Mexico territory, Mexico and Texas to the eastern banks of the Rio Grande, which was the only water course of importance. Nearby, the southern ranges approached nearer the river valley. The Organ mountains lay less than twenty miles east. Although unique in appearance, they did not derive their name from a fancied resemblance to any musical mechanism, but from the Orajons, a once numerous tribe of Indians who inhabited the region in the early days, he had learned. The Spanish word, Orajon, means 'long ears', and was given to the tribe on account of the physical peculiarity of its members.

He had travelled all over this part of the world, or so it felt. The plains of the country furnished an abundance of grass for beef cattle. He was considering settling down to raise his own herds. That was the type of woman Nina Marie Romero was to him.

He had only wished he had come to that realization sooner.

She too had come all the long way from a green, plush valley in New Mexico to return him home, but now she lay dying in the heat, disease and the indifference of Old Mexico while the man who loved her stood over her with a face the colour of school house chalk.

'The fever,' intoned the ancient medico, turning back her eyelid with gnarled but steady fingers. He sat back and sighed. 'The *señorita*'s passing shall take the number of those to die in Hermanas Pozos this evil month to ten.' Another, but longer, sigh. 'So goes this world.'

With enormous effort, Cotton Harding dragged his eyes away from Nina Marie Romero's feverish face to focus on the old man beside him.

'Eleven,' he breathed.

Doctor Hector Colón stared uncomprehendingly at the tall *gringo* mercenary. The fat woman serving as his nurse also stared. So did the old man waiting to have his broken fingers splinted, and the boy who had brought in a bottle of Tequila in case either the patient or the doctor needed a good stiff drink.

Nobody understood.

'*¿Qué?*' grunted the doctor. 'What is it you say, *señor?*'

Suddenly, he found his skinny old legs dangling as Cotton Harding lifted him out of his chair by his lapels.

'If she dies, you greasy fraud,' he grated, 'then so will you. You'll be number eleven!'

The change this information made was dramatic. Doc Colón, the long-faced pessimist of mere moments ago, was now a bright-eyed optimist as he buzzed around the sickbed calling for cold cloths, a fan and certain medications, which he assured Harding were the very latest scientific developments. When he saw Harding rubbing a bronzed thumb along the ivory butt of his Colt .45, he even sent the kid outside with instructions to pour water over the roof to lower the temperature inside.

All of Hermanas Pozos sweltered that day, but on the roof of that building standing between the cantina and the mercantile store, the temperature stood at broiling heat. The kid hopped from one bare foot to the other as he splashed the roof with water. The hot metal sizzled and dried instantly. The boy wished the *gringo* woman had perished before Harding had reached Hermanas Pozos. He felt like telling both the doctor and the *gringo* to go straight to hell when he climbed back down, but Doctor Colón paid him just enough to keep himself and his crippled mother alive. And the tall *gringo* scared him. Sighing, he went to fetch more water.

Inside the building, the old doctor talked without

ceasing, for fear that silence might lead to violence.

'. . . the fever, *señor*, is endemic to this region – always waiting in the soil itself and in the water . . .' the Mexican doctor tried to explain.

'Get more water!' Harding shouted angrily through the window. 'Stir your stumps, or you will be wearin' that pail for a hat, kid!'

Rolling his eyes at his plump nurse, Colón peeled off his dirty and shabby black coat, fitted a stethoscope to hairy ears and listened in on an erratic heartbeat. Thump . . . thump . . . thump-thump! The double beat wasn't good. Sometimes it could precede the end.

'Saints protect me!' he whispered, sweating like a fever victim himself, dabbing his forehead with his coat sleeve. Then he added almost as an afterthought, 'And also the poor, pretty *señorita*, of course.'

Cotton Harding grew wary and paced up and down behind him liked a caged animal. A man on the edge.

They had been lovers before Cotton Harding rode off into Mexico in search of his fortune – more like to earn it with his gun. He told her that he would be back within a year, but that year became two, and then he was well into the third. He was by then a hard-bitten *gringo* with a quick gun, even quicker temper, a good sorrel horse and hordes of good friends and bitter enemies – but still with no fortune.

The money had always slipped through his grasp before he could make it back to Kettle Springs, New Mexico, and the woman he loved who was waiting for him.

At various times in his life, Cotton Harding had been rich, poor, shot-up, lonesome, living high on the hog, sentenced to hang and riding at the head of a two hundred strong rebel army during the Battle of Dranesville in the war between the states. He left that mess, became fluent in Spanish and earned a reputation as a good man with a .45 who was mortally hard to kill. He was also known as a man who did not mess with women.

'He's got a gal back in the States,' his fellow gun partners would say, and never a week went by that Cotton did not set himself down with paper and pen and get a letter off to Kettle Springs, a letter which always finished with the words, '*Love you and see you soon. . . .*'

It was never intended to be a lie.

It had been two years, four months, two weeks and three days. That was the exact length of time Nina Marie Romero waited before presenting herself before one sun-bronzed soldier of fortune with her ultimatum all ready for delivery: 'Either you come home and marry me right now, or it's all over between us. . . .'

But Nina Marie never had to say those words. She did not have to say anything. The moment Cotton Harding saw her, he realized what a bullet-headed fool he had been the past two plus years. He took his girl in his arms and told her they were leaving immediately for a better part of New Mexico or perhaps further West to Arizona or California.

And so they did. They went north, as happy and carefree as any two lovers could ever be, but the sickness was in Nina Marie Romero's bloodstream and multiplying with every passing second. By the time they were following the trail along The Nape, that long, narrow stretch of stone separating the twin blue lakes, she was hallucinating, sweating profusely and begging her love, Cotton, not to let her die.

'She *can't* die!' Cotton Harding's voice raged in Hermanas Pozos' velvet darkness that night.

For the very first time since coming to Mexico, he entered one of the little churches and was overwhelmed with the smells of incense, candle wax and mortal sin. The gunfighter and all those who saw him blessed themselves and set their rosaries fairly humming.

It was after ten o'clock when Cotton left the *cantina* and stepped into the tiny square. Force of long habit compelled him to test the warm darkness with eyes, ears and nose. It was awfully quiet in Hermanas Pozos, a town where most citizens left their beds long before dawn for a long day's work in the fields.

The serrated rooftops and battered old church tower fanged the night sky. Here and there, the silhouette of a ruined building showed against bright stars. Hermanas Pozos had seen its share of trouble, and then some. It was the Law of the Strong in this section of Old Mexico, and Hermanas Pozos, like so many similar places in the region, was weak. Exploited by the bloated landowners and preyed upon by brigands and bandits, Hermanas Pozos could rightly be termed a town of tears, even by Mexico's harsh standards.

A horse clattered over the narrow little bridge and thudded on the hard-packed street. Although Cotton Harding's thoughts were centred in a little metal-roofed hospital, he was still alert and still kept one hand close to his gun butt as he stared down the dark street, waiting for the horseman to appear. He wasn't expecting trouble – no one ever truly did – on the dusty square of Hermanas Pozos, but he had seen many a good man die when he wasn't expecting it.

Harding was tall and impressive. His nose was short and his chin long. The Mexican sun had made its mark on him with lines at the corners of his clear blue eyes. His dark brown hair had kept its colour only because his Stetson covered it. His clothes were plain enough, but the six-guns were things of beauty – ivory handled .45s in hand-tooled leather holsters. The leather matched his tan boots. He was the kind of man you wouldn't brace unless you were mighty sure of yourself, or tired of living.

The horseman rode into the light. A peon on a roach-backed pony. He rode like a man with the worries of the world on his shoulders. Cotton Harding shook his head and moved on. The Mexican probably had a plump, healthy wife waiting for him at home. Not every man was that lucky.

The Mexican man dismounted and entered the cantina, leaving Cotton Harding to kill time until his next visit to the hospital and his love.

A light still burned in the front window of the old house. A soft rectangle of gold spilled into the dusty, wind blown street. Within the house, a man laughed softly. In Mexico, the nights belonged either to love or to violence. Now Harding was a lover again. He wondered if that old sawbones really knew what he was talking about. Too bad if he did not. The next nearest doctor was over a hundred miles away.

Cotton Harding worked his way around the houses, cursing softly as he kicked through piles of garbage and refuse. He would never grow used to Mexico's filth. A burro brayed as he passed a peeled-pole corral. Somewhere across the town, a dog barked.

When he reached the town's plaza he saw there were more lights showing than before, even though it was now close to midnight. Men at one time worked from sun-up to sundown raising cattle and tending farms. The area around Hermanas Pozos was a place where cattle and sheep flourished on the gramma grass that grew luxuriantly on thousands of acres of land unfit for cultivation. The warm winters made it unnecessary to provide shelter or hay for feed. Near larger towns, dairy farms made a large profit, as milk, butter and cheese were in great demand.

Now the men had gathered in the square in groups – talking, gesturing, waving lighted cigarettes.

24

It was strange to see so many people out and about, but he could not be less interested. He had told them at the hospital he would not be back until after midnight, but found that he could not wait a second longer. He had to see his Nina Marie. He had to know. . . .

He found Doctor Hector Colón sitting outside on the stoop, talking in the air and sipping tequila. . . .

'The drink of heroes,' he said almost with a grin, but then thought better of it, hefting the glass. 'Would you like some, *señor*?'

'Another red-blooded hero in this town might overbalance it,' was Cotton's sardonic reply. He had to pause to get up the courage to ask, 'How – how is she? How is Nina Marie?'

'Much the same, I'm afraid. . . .' Colón held his glass up to the light, and it was with a sense of shock that Cotton Harding realized the medicine man was flat drunk.

'But what does it matter now?' the doctor shrugged. 'Soon we shall all of us be dead. . . .'

In that moment, Doctor Hector Colón of Hermanas Pozos was a single heartbeat away from death. Harding dashed the glass from the old man's hand and shoved a gun barrel into his skinny guts as he reefed him to his feet.

'That about does it!' Harding threatened. 'From here on in, old man, I'm stickin' to you like a second skin. I'm goin' to be with you twenty-four hours a day, and if you so much as sniff a drink, I will kill you on the spot, *comprendes*?'

'Better hurry, *gringo*,' the medicine man replied.

A puzzled frown cut Harding's brows as he loosened his grip. There was something wrong here, he realized. The little old man was afraid of something – but not of him. He could smell the fear, like the air coming out of an ice house doorway.

'What in the hell are you talkin' about?' Harding demanded of the man.

Doc Colón hiccuped, and then he simply said, 'Juan Manuel Benitez comes again.'

CHAPTER 2

NO TOWN FOR HEROES

The lieutenant of the town of La Tenajo had fled when the bandito army first poured into his town at dusk. Now, in the morning's small hours, he was returning, reassured by the sounds of singing and revelry, convinced that he could rally his people and hurl the *alimañas* – the vermin – out.

The lieutenant had drunk much *pulque* – fermented agave cactus juice – to bolster his courage. His steps were uncertain as he left his weary horse, but he managed a certain stiff-necked dignity as he made his way to the town square. He heard the sounds of guitars and drums and loud voices in the air. He squared his shoulders and lifted his head and held his chunky body erect as befitted a man of the law. He held his sabre firmly before him as a symbol

27

of his authority.

As soon as he set foot in the town plaza, he was surrounded by brigands who were intimidated neither by his dignity nor his sword. They spat on him and cuffed him. The enraged lieutenant lifted his sabre and slashed a man's arm to the bone in one bloody swoosh.

That was the last mistake he made.

They were playing football with the lieutenant's head when bandit leader Juan Manuel Benitez rode into the town at daybreak.

Although Cotton Harding knew a lot about Juan Manuel Benitez, he knew very little about the connection between Benitez and Hermanas Pozos. The terrified locals were able to fill in the gaps for him.

Juan Manuel Benitez was the leader of a swarm of outlaws known as *El Azotar* – the Scourge. They had plagued that region of Mexico for the past several years. After leaving prison, Juan Manuel Benitez joined with Juan Flores and a dozen or so ranch hands, miners and others like Chino Fontes, 'One-eyed' Cartabo, Jesus Garcia, Anastasia Varelas and Faustino Espinoza, to name a few.

Their victims in the main were the poor and unarmed. The gang's specialty was the surprise raid on small towns. Plunder and rape were inevitable penalties for failure to pay what Juan Manuel Benitez demanded.

Five years earlier, so Cotton Harding learned over several stiff tequilas in Flo's Cantina, Benitez swept off the grain plains to attack Hermanas Pozos and her sister towns of La Tenajo and Santa Rosa, both situated south, further than most Americans would go into Mexico. Although Hermanas Pozos showed some resistance, it was to no avail. There were at least thirty new graves in the town's little cemetery and a dozen ruined buildings when Juan Manuel Benitez finally rode on, carrying off two of the town's most beautiful maidens.

After that raid, the townsfolk of the region formed an alliance designed to give them unity through strength when and if *El Azotar* came again.

'I've got a hunch they did come back,' Harding said without rolling his eyes.

He, of course, was right.

Rumours spread that Juan Manuel Benitez was being driven by the largest force ever mounted against him. There was panic at first, but then the three towns' leaders went into council and laid plans for their defence.

It was quickly learned that, due to the relentless harassment of the law, The Scourge were in desperate need of supplies as any army of size needed. They wanted weapons, ammunition, fresh horses, medical attention and food. Most of all, they needed food. . . .

The town leaders gave their orders, and overnight, the granaries, orchards and farmyards of the region were stripped bare. The produce was transported into the towns, where people who had never even handled weapons before took up guns to protect themselves from the raiders.

The cream of the able-bodied men from Hermanas Pozos and Santa Rosa rode off to La Tenajo to be on hand when The Scourge showed over the southern horizon, daunted by long weeks on the run.

Astonishingly, the first wave of outlaws was driven off, as was the second and third.

Juan Manuel Benitez was enraged by what he called 'treachery' from people who had assisted him before, even if it had been against their will. He was preparing for the full-scale annihilation of La Tenajo when his pursuers caught up with him and put him to flight.

In the week that followed, The Scourge were scattered across the plains, both by the *Federales* and by their own, desperate search for food.

They beat against the walls of Hermanas Pozos and Santa Rosa, but due to their hunger and lack of organization and to the stubborn durability of the defenders, they failed to breach the defences. Finally, they were scattered by Juan Manuel Benitez.

Benitez survived, of course, carrying into his mountain exile the corpse of his son. The youth had been slain in an attack on Hermanas Pozos.

Now nearly six months later, new rumours began to trickle to the plains: Juan Manuel Benitez was on the move once more; *El Azolar* had reformed and were growing stronger by the day; Juan Manuel Benitez had promised to deal with all the 'traitors' who had turned on him in his desperate hour, and especially with the triple towns of Santa Rosa, Hermanas Pozos and La Tenajo.

There were also rumours that he carried in his saddlebags the skull of his dead son, which he had vowed to set atop the church tower in Hermanas Pozos for all to see – before putting the torch to the town and everyone in it.

Real fear ate away at the three towns as time went by and stories of Scourge atrocities in far regions continued to filter through. The militia of the three towns continued to meet and train on a regular basis, but their hearts weren't in it. Last time they had taken Juan Manuel Benitez by surprise with their well-planned resistance. As well, *El Azotar* had been sorely harried and eventually routed by a combined force of *Federales* and *Rurales*.

No such force existed now. Rifts and schisms had set the law forces at loggerheads. Border wars and internal strife ensured that they were too preoccupied to concern themselves over something as flimsy as a rumour of Juan Manuel Benitez's return.

Now he had struck. The chilling news that he was on his way from the south had reached Hermanas Pozos by the same messenger who reported that La Tenajo had already fallen, with death and destruction stalking its streets and public squares. The town and its people were virtually gone – erased off the map by this madman and his army of bandits.

'Santa Rosa shall be next,' quavered the major of Hermanas Pozos, 'but The Scourge shall save their real fury for us. It was not one hundred yards from

where we now stand that Juan Manuel Benitez's son
fell with a bullet through his brain.' He shuddered
and looked ashen as he continued. 'He shall be
avenged.'

Cotton Harding stared around in disgust at the
spectacle of grown men shaking in their boots and
trying to dull the edges of harsh reality with liquor at
a time that called for clear heads and purposeful
action. He expected to see puddles of urine under
each of their feet.

'Mexicans!' he sneered. 'Gutless... all of you! Fight
for your town!'

They were too afraid to resent the remark, but
they could still be hurt nonetheless.

'It is different for you, *señor*,' said the clever-faced
young man named Eugenio, who seemed to be held
in high regard by most in the town. 'You, a *gringo pistolero* with a big, fast horse. You can be long gone
before Juan Manuel Benitez comes. Surely, he shall
take his time so that we may suffer as much from
fearing what is coming as from what does come in
the end. But where can we run to? The plains? The
Scourge would hunt us down and kill us like wild
animals. To Don José Antonio Parra to ask for sanc-
tuary? No. Parra and Benitez fear and respect each
other and therefore do nothing to give offence.'
Eugenio shrugged and added, 'What we do is stay
here and wait like the chicken awaiting the axe. We
accept it, but we do not deserve your contempt.'

'You fought 'em once, why not again?' Cotton
snapped back with contempt.

'We have just told you how different things were then, *amigo*,' said the mayor.

'Uh huh. So you are goin' to fall down and play dead dog? Well, I always say that any man who won't fight is bound to die.' He drained his glass and then fitted his hat to his head. 'See you when the grapes get ripe – heroes!'

'Where do you go, *amigo*?' the mayor asked wistfully, as though picturing himself crossing the great plains on a fast horse pointed to New Mexico or further north. 'North?' he made it sound like 'heaven'.

'Damn right,' Harding fired back. 'So, who's goin' to sell me a good covered wagon?'

'You go by wagon?' asked Odalis, a buxom lady who had removed her pearl necklace and replaced it with a string of rosary beads when she heard the bad news of the town's impending doom.

'*Amigo*,' she went on, crossing herself, 'even if you are a brave *pistolero* and do not feel fear as we do, you should not be so slow in leaving. They say that The Scourge may not come for ten days, but who knows? They may come tonight. And their swift horses will run down any wagon.'

'I've got a sick woman with me,' Cotton Harding said shortly, and then he nodded to a fat man with a pale face. 'You got a wagon? I will pay you fifty American dollars for it.' He put on a cruel grin. 'Looks like you won't be needin' it where you are goin'... *amigo*.'

The man sold him the wagon, and Cotton used up

most of what was left of his dwindling supply of cash in outfitting it with bedding and harnessing the rig to the best two mules left in town.

The sooner he could get out of this town and country, the better it would be for Nina Marie and him, he reasoned.

Then came the big blow. Doc Colón told him something that Harding should have figured out for himself.

The medicine man told him in no uncertain terms that to even think of moving the patient in her present condition would kill her as quickly as putting a gun to her head.

He would either have to leave her or stay with her.

CHAPTER 3

JUAN MANUEL BENITEZ RIDES

The flames of the town of La Tenajo made the night sky as bright as day for Juan Manuel Benitez and his lieutenants as they rested in the plaza. The leader stroked the gleaming human skull standing on the bench before him. He looked up and laughed as a citizen, his clothing ablaze, jumped from a second floor window of the hotel to the ground below. He landed with a loud thud.

His laughter was taken up by all within earshot. When Juan Manuel Benitez was entertained, all were entertained. When Juan Manuel Benitez suffered, everybody suffered.

The man looked like the brigand he was – over sized, overweight, hairy, noisy, oily and dirty. An atrocity on horseback. A Mexican nightmare who killed to live and lived to kill.

'Burn, traitors, burn!' he roared with laughter, banging the table so hard with his fist the skull overturned. 'Hey, my Marco, do you not laugh when you see what befalls those who turned against us?' the brigand asked.

The grinning skull did indeed seem to be laughing as Juan Manuel Benitez turned it towards the flames.

Although most of the *El Azotar* were more animal than human, there were still many who shuddered at the leader's habit of transporting his son's skull around and addressing it as though it was alive. But it entertained Juan Manuel Benitez, and whatever achieved that end was to be commended, for Juan Manuel Benitez in an evil temper was a mortal danger – even more so than his other moods.

A parade of young virgins were dragged into the plaza, and for some time, Juan Manuel Benitez was occupied selecting the girls whose 'privilege' it would be to share his bed.

Juan Manuel Benitez smacked his lips and slugged down a glass of tequila as he watched his selections being led away.

'They were children a few years ago,' Juan Manuel Benitez told his henchmen, his sweaty, swarthy face undergoing a remarkable change from salacious pleasure to slit-eyed hatred. 'Little children who cheered their fathers when they kept us from their gates.' He kicked a chair, sending it far out into the plaza. 'Now they are women, and I will enjoy them while their fathers hang from the church tower.' He rammed a huge fist into the air. '¡*Viva Azotar!*'

The chant was taken up until the square rang with it. Juan Manuel Benitez had hated the name people had placed on his raiders initially, but had eventually embraced it in a spirit of defiant bravado. Particularly over the past two years as the band had come back from the brink of extinction to grow stronger than ever before, the very name '*Azotar*' had become in itself a shock weapon to terrorize people and bring them to their knees without a shot even being fired.

When the poor citizens of La Tenajo had looked up from the evening meal to see their square flooding with wild-eyed, pistol shooting hellions, chanting, '¡*Azotar! ¡Azotar! ¡Viva Azotar!*' at the top of their lungs, they were already virtually defeated.

Suddenly the chant changed, and the barbarians were hooting, 'Here comes the mayor!'

Mayor Guzman had been found hiding beneath a bed in the priest's house. He was a great prize, for the mayor had been the originator of the three-town union that had caused The Scourge such grief.

By the glow of burning buildings, the face of the bandit king Juan Manuel Benitez showed a malevolent pleasure. The mayor still wore his robes of office. He had been attempting to rally the townsfolk to defend La Tenajo when the first of the Azotar came galloping into the square.

'So, the famous hero,' Juan Manuel Benitez said,

now nursing the skull of his son in his lap. 'And where is your resistance, now? Huh?'

The mayor dropped to his knees in a desperate attempt for mercy.

'Señor Juan Manuel Benitez, have mercy,' the mayor begged shamelessly. 'In the name of the Virgin. . . .'

'Do you hear that, Marco?' Juan Manuel Benitez asked the grinning skull. 'Mercy in the Virgin's name, eh? It would seem I remember only too well beseeching Her to save your life when you were shot. . . .' He paused to finger the gaping, splintered bullet hole in the forehead of the skull. '. . . But all to no avail. . . .' He shook himself and spoke briskly again. 'So why should a holy Virgin who denied a loving father the life of his sweet son turn around and favour a miserable, cowardly, fat pig of a mayor? *Compañeros*, can you tell me why?'

Juan Manuel Benitez and the mayor were surrounded now by a sea of savage faces; gaunt faces, bloated faces, the faces of butchers and those of the truly depraved. Scourge by name and villainous by nature, these were the sweepings of the rat holes of Mexico, and even those who had not been part of the previous, ill-fated raid on the three towns were filled with venom towards the sweating fat man.

Like puppets, the killers shook their heads and the kneeling mayor was dragged to his feet by a Juan Manuel Benitez lieutenant with arms like cured hams.

'Now?' the muscular brute asked, pressing the

point of his dagger against the mayor's throat.

'Marco says it must be slow,' intoned Benitez. 'And painful. My son is just like his old man.'

'*Por favor*, great Juan Manuel Benitez,' the mayor begged, 'you have been misinformed. It was not I who created the union of the towns. I was but a tool used by Santa Rosa and Hermanas Pozos to help in their defence. . . .'

Juan Manuel Benitez back-handed him to the ground. The leader was diverted for a moment as a blood-curdling scream echoed across the square. All turned to see two mounted raiders pursuing a blind man stumbling past the cantina, where seven citizens hung from the rafters. The man was blind because the raiders had put out his eyes before letting him go. The horsemen were deliberately herding him into the inferno of the La Tenajo Hotel.

Juan Manuel Benitez returned his attention to the mayor, who had got back to his feet.

'There is but one reason why your three miserable towns were not ready to do battle with us again as you did before,' he snarled, 'and that is because I gave you no time to do so. I told my heroes that when we returned here, we should strike like the lightning bolt, and this we have done. As you can see with your own eyes, La Tenajo is no more. My men are also converging on Santa Rosa at this very moment to sow the seeds of panic.'

'I kiss your hand, great Juan Manuel Benitez,' the mayor offered.

The mayor tried to do just that, but Juan Manuel

Benitez kneed him in the groin and watched him squirm helplessly on the ground.

Juan Manuel Benitez's eyes had a distant look as he addressed his men – The Scourge.

'There will be much sport in Santa Rosa, my heroes. We shall not put it quickly to the torch as we have this foul hole. Instead, we shall fully enjoy its fruits ... while Hermanas Pozos dies a thousand times waiting for us to come. ...'

Staring up from the ground with pain-filled eyes, the mayor saw how Juan Manuel Benitez's face came alive at mention of Hermanas Pozos.

'It ... it was the citizens of Hermanas Pozos who conceived of the union, not I, great Juan Manuel Benitez,' he panted, adding lies to his cowardice now. 'I opposed the idea but was forced to join.' He clutched at Juan Manuel Benitez's baggy trousers and hauled himself up again as he said, 'I have a brilliant strategy, great leader. Allow me to go to Hermanas Pozos. I shall persuade them to offer no resistance so that you will be free to ride in and deal with them as you will without the loss of so much as one man.'

Juan Manuel Benitez's laughter started from his boots. It trembled his tree-trunk-like legs and worked its way up his huge body until he was shaking all over. The skull tucked beneath one arm jiggled to his movements, almost as if it had come to life.

The mayor was offering to betray his own people, to do anything, just so that he might survive. Juan Manuel Benitez, who regarded himself as a man of impeccable courage, was filled with towering, cynical contempt for the weakness of others.

'A generous offer,' he said mockingly, 'as Marco agrees. But your assistance is not necessary. As I said, our plan is to give Hermanas Pozos time to suffer every agony of expectation before we come knocking on the city door.' He stroked the skull. 'Perhaps we shall linger in Santa Rosa for as long as a week while Hermanas Pozos' citizens suffer the agonies of the damned. They will try to run, try to organize a defence... even fall to fighting among themselves and blaming one another, as desperate men all do eventually.' He thrust a finger into the smoky air. 'This for us will be the true revenge. Wiping them off the face of the earth is a mere formality.'

Juan Manuel Benitez turned to the mayor and gave a small bow. 'So,' he said softly, 'grateful as I am for your offer, you can see that your help is not necessary.'

A fleeting eye signal passed between Juan Manuel Benitez and the muscular bandit who stood behind the mayor. As the mayor held out an entreating hand, a machete flashed. The hand fell to the earth.

Immediately, another two men leapt upon the ashen faced mayor, one to hold his other arm imprisoned while the other slashed off the remaining hand causing blood to squirt out onto his boots and the ground.

The raider waved the bloody hand in the mayor's face, laughing all the while.

'This hand will never withhold food from a

41

Scourge again,' the bandit leader shouted.

A machete slashed downwards, hacking off a foot. Frenzied now, the raiders swarmed around the stricken man, chopping and slashing as they accused him of crimes against The Scourge.

'*¡Jesu-Cristo!*' the mayor cried out in unbearable agony. 'Give me strength and courage. Forgive me my sins.'

'He may forgive you, but we never shall,' screamed Juan Manuel Benitez as a one-eyed hellion pried open the mayor's mouth and tore out his tongue.

Others gouged out his eyes and cut off his ears from his head. Juan Manuel Benitez was holding his belly against the pain of his laughter as an over-eager outlaw plunged a knife into the mayor's heart and brought the night's entertainment to an end.

CHAPTER 4

THE COYOTE
CANNOT HALT
THE WOLF

Her pulse was weak, and her skin hot to the touch. Cotton Harding gently brushed a damp cloth across Nina Marie's brow and smoothed back the soft, dark hair.

'She's worse, isn't she?' he grated. 'Come on, doctor, you don't have to lie to me. I can take it.'

He plainly could not take it, so Doc Colón lied. 'The *señorita* is improving, *señor*. . . .'

He broke off when he saw the savage look Cotton directed at him. The room was quiet as the tall American rose from his bedside chair. Cotton Harding was pale beneath his tan, and beads of sweat stood out on his face as he stood staring down at the woman in the bed. He was seeing her as she was when she came to meet him – vibrant, bright-eyed, running to him without hesitation. She had travelled five hundred miles alone to find him, and just one embrace was all it took to convince one tough soldier of fortune what a fool he had been for so long.

He had been happy in the short time before she fell ill, maybe happier than ever in his life. No more hiring his gun to the highest bidder. No more gun-running, smuggling, body-guarding arrogant Spanish landlords or enforcing 'laws' with a .45 in a way that only *gringo pistoleros* seemed capable of doing. Harding was heading back home to New Mexico with his sweetheart, to raise corn and children and to forget his greedy dreams.

But that was all over now. He was unhappier than he had ever been. It showed in the rough way he elbowed the Mexican boy out of his path and jostled two patients waiting to see the doctor.

There was resentment in the faces that watched Harding make his long-legged, slim-hipped way across the square. They resented *gringos* down here, especially his kind. Harding's kind came to Mexico like conquerors. They were taller, meaner, faster with a gun and better on horses than most of the local men. They had money. They worked for the wealthy and powerful. They came only for the big rewards available to hard men who were not too particular about the way they earned a dollar. In just about every way that mattered, Cotton Harding was typical of his breed, right down to his obvious contempt for ordinary Mexicans.

Harding ordered tequila in the town's cantina, but he did not drink it. His shirt was soaked in sweat. He swabbed his forehead and stared up at the slow-moving hands of the ancient clock above the bar.

Time was running out on his happiness . . . on everything . . . on her!

He whirled suddenly to confront the drinkers and gamblers who were continuing to while away their time as they always did, despite the cloud hovering over their town.

'Why aren't you doin' something?' he shouted at them. 'Anything. Why aren't you diggin' trenches or buildin' breastworks or even offerin' to buy The Scourge off? I swear you're just like cows in a slaughterhouse. You know what's comin', but you just sit there waitin' for it. You're worse than cows. They put up a fight sometimes.'

His scathing words had no visible effect. Narrow-shouldered, care-worn men stared back at him in the cool gloom of the smoky *cantina*. They were people for whom such things as disaster, defeat and subservience were the norm. They were not heroes. Just once, the people of the three towns had become something more. A unique set of circumstances gave them the chance to stand up against a murderous raider.

None of those circumstances prevailed now, and Hermanas Pozos knew it was doomed. There were no soldiers and no early warnings. The union of the three towns had crumbled the moment El Azotar attacked La Tenajo. Now, with rumours that Santa

Rosa was also under assault, Hermanas Pozos knew it was completely on its own. The Scourge were reported to be two-hundred strong. The men of Hermanas Pozos stared dull-eyed at the *gringo* mercenary and wished he would go away so they could grieve in peace, while there was still time.

But Cotton Harding knew now the fate of Hermanas Pozos was his fate – his and Nina Marie's. If the town went under, they would go with it.

'It could be done,' he declared, adopting a more persuasive tone. 'Hermanas Pozos is in a good position to defend itself against an attack from the south. I swear, it is true. You might think I am pullin' your leg just because I want to talk you into this, but that's not the case. Just a handful of men could keep *El Azotar* at bay forever if they had grit enough. Do you want me to tell you how?'

They did not apparently.

Every evening now, a crowd lined up at the confessional in the little church. Hermanas Pozos was making its communal peace with its Creator. It was preparing for the inevitable, and the inevitable was their deaths.

'The Nape!' Harding said loudly.

He snatched up the bartender's chalk and strode to the wall facing the bat-wings.

'Here, I will show you . . .' he added.

With urgent strokes, he drew a diagram that resembled a woman's hourglass figure. To the left and right of the narrow waist, he scrawled a circle.

'The Twin Lakes,' he said unnecessarily to men

who had been born and raised within an hour's ride of the place. Then he jabbed his chalk at the diagram's 'waist'. 'And here, The Nape – about five-hundred yards long and about a hundred wide, the only way through.' He tapped the chalk repeatedly, creating a series of dots. 'Right there. That's where they can be stopped . . . and I reckon every mother's son of you knows this to be the truth. . . .'

He broke off as the doors opened and the mayor and the youthful Eugenio came in.

Although Cotton Harding had already dismissed the mayor as a coward and blow-hard, he was inclined to take Eugenio seriously. Although only in his late teens or early twenties, Eugenio seemed to be regarded as the town's most level-headed man. He was a ragged peasant like the others, but more thoughtful. His words carried weight. Harding sensed that in order to persuade the town to take any course of action, he would first need to persuade this bright-eyed young man.

He repeated his little lecture for the benefit of the newcomers. The result was not encouraging. The mayor went to the bar to order a drink. Eugenio dropped into a chair, tilted it backwards and shook his head.

'The chicken cannot stop the fox, Señor Harding,' Eugenio said finally. 'Not even at The Nape.' A shrug. 'Not even anywhere.'

Cotton Harding cursed. He cajoled. He asked them if they had heard of the tale of Horatio and the bridge. They did not respond.

So Harding told them the tale: 'Horatio was a mythical Roman hero credited with saving Rome from Etruscan invaders in the 500s BC. According to the legend, Horatio led a group of warriors who were defending the Sublician Bridge, which led across the Tiber River into Rome. He ordered his troops to take down the bridge, while he and two companions fought off the Etruscans. Horatio sent these men back over the bridge just before it collapsed. As the bridge fell, he jumped into the Tiber while still wearing his armour and swam to safety.'

Still no response from the men.

He drew more diagrams to show entrenched defenders covering The Nape with rifles. He talked tactics and worked himself into a sweat extolling the virtues of courageous resistance over meek capitulation. He ended up throwing the chalk at one man who had fallen asleep during his performance, and then he retired to retrieve his neglected tequila.

As he stared at his reflection in the mirror, his eyes suddenly brightened with one last hope. He realized that he had overlooked something that was of vital importance to every Mexican, even the cowards.

'Money!' he shouted, swinging to face them. '*Dinero.* You will fight for money. Right?'

For a moment, there seemed to be some flicker of interest. To a Mexican who might live and die without once knowing the luxury of a full belly, money was magical. Poor peons never seemed to have any, but a certain breed of *gringo* never seemed to be without it.

And so he finished the tale he had started, 'Horatio's bravery saved Rome from invasion, the city erected a statue of him and gave him a large amount of land as a reward.'

Then the moment had passed by, and the eyes were turning away. It was too late for money. What good was it to a man hanging by his heels over an *Azotar* bonfire?

Eugenio crossed the room to join Cotton Harding.

'There is no money, Señor Harding,' he said in a resigned tone that only somebody of Spanish blood seemed able to master. 'There is only hardship, toil, sickness, a little pleasure perhaps if one is lucky . . . and there is death. That is all we have here.'

'There's money all right,' retorted Harding, ignoring the young man's assertions, his mind racing. 'And I can get my hands on it. . . .' He paused momentarily, a little awed by what he was thinking. Then he shook his head, realizing that he had no choice but to take every risk in the book. 'More money than this rat trap town has ever seen. Can you talk them into it, boy? I don't want to get myself killed tryin' to get money if it's no use to me. Would they fight?'

'Ah, *señor*, these people have been fighting all their lives,' Eugenio said.

Nina Marie is dying, Harding thought a little heavy-hearted. *She is dying, Juan Manuel Benitez is on his way, and I am standin' in a bar, listenin' to a young Mexican philosopher.*

He forced himself to remain calm; it was harder

than he expected.

'Why don't you talk 'em into it while I go get the money, Eugenio?' He jerked his chin towards the wall opposite the door, where two weary looking men were studying his diagrams. 'This town could be defended at The Nape if we could just muster enough men, and you know it.'

'You want *hombres* to leave their loved ones to their fate while they go and die at the lakes?' Eugenio shook his head sadly in resignation. 'It is an impossible thing you ask.' Then he lifted his brows. 'Just as the money is impossible, I think.'

'I can get the money, damn you!' Harding insisted.

'Where?' the youth smiled. 'Do you steal it, *gringo*?'

He was joking, but the truth was that he was dead on target. Harding had never stolen, but now he was ready to steal, burn or kill. And he knew that was the only way he would get Don José Antonio Parra to part with a little of his wealth.

'Can you persuade them?' he demanded.

He was pleading now and honestly it was making him nauseous. He could not stand off two-hundred unwashed barbarians alone. He had to have help. He gave in and tried flattery.

'The people look up to you. They respect you. You owe it to them to show leadership when they need it most,' Harding reasoned.

'If they respect me, it is because I never expect them to do the impossible or the foolish,' the young man replied.

'Then you call fightin' to save yourselves foolish?'

'Perhaps we can pay Juan Manuel Benitez tribute and he will spare us?' offered Eugenio.

'Why, you yellow-bellied greaser, you're no better than the rest of 'em,' shouted Harding.

'Why do you hate Mexicans, Señor Harding?' asked Eugenio.

'Who says I hate Mexicans?' Harding demanded to know.

'It shows in everything you say and do. You do not care for the safety of Hermanas Pozos, *señor*. We could all die, and you would not shed a single tear. You wish for us to fight because you fear for your woman. You are a selfish man who thinks only of himself, and we all know it. That is why no man will fight for you, not because we are afraid,' Eugenio explained simply.

'Son of a bitch!' Harding hissed as he headed for the bat-wings.

He was at the bedside minutes later, and a few minutes after that, he was saddling his horse as a lathered rider arrived in town from the south.

The news he brought with him was grim. The Scourge had burned the town of La Tenajo to the ground, and now Santa Rosa was encircled. One ray of hope came for Cotton Harding. The weary messenger related a rumour that the bandit king Juan Manuel Benitez was in no hurry to sack Hermanas Pozos, that he wanted the town to suffer every agony of fear and anticipation before his vengeful Scourge were unleashed.

Cotton Harding needed all the time he could get.

51

CHAPTER 5

LONG MILES TO SAN CRISTÓBAL

It was Don José Antonio Parra country for as far as Cotton Harding could see and for as long as anybody could remember. A vast, rolling sweep of prime farmlands and prime graze extended on all sides of the solitary, stealthy figure that walked a narrow roadway between fields of head-high corn. There was enough land and riches to support a thousand here, but every inch and peso of it was clenched tightly in the fist of Don José Antonio Parra.

Don José's ranch was in an area of rugged mountain terrain in the Chihuahuan Desert, where scrub, sotol, cacti, and sparse grasses grow.

San Cristóbal Ranch boasted several rivers, its own mountain range, a small town populated by *vaqueros*, farm labourers and their families. There were huge herds of cattle. The Europeans who first settled in America at the end of the fifteenth century had brought longhorn cattle with them. By the early nineteenth century cattle ranches were common in Mexico.

There was timber country where axes rang from daylight to dusk. The *hacienda* at the heart of it all was the last word in luxury and a dazzling contrast to the hovels in which so many of Don José's people were forced to live.

That great house was Cotton Harding's only target. He headed for it on foot, with his face and hands blackened by charcoal to reduce the risk of being sighted by the Don's nighthawks.

The rich man was closely guarded. He had many enemies and much wealth, and that was always a risky combination in Old Mexico.

Harding knew Don José Antonio Parra. Had worked for him once, but now he walked Don José's rich acres in an unfamiliar role – as an enemy.

It was mid evening when he reached the head-quarters. He knew where the guards were positioned, and he sought them out one by one. He dealt with the first man with a swift efficiency – a thump across the skull with a six-gun and then into a storage shed with the unconscious form. The second sentry proved no more difficult than the first, but the third gave Harding a heart-stopping moment when he got off half a yell before the six-gun barrel made crunching contact with his hard head.

Cotton Harding sweated as he crouched in the

shadows and waited. Someone emerged from the mansion, listened for a few moments and then returned back inside.

It was about then that Harding sensed he might make it – being new to this type of illicit activity. Until that time, he had been skin-full of doubts. Better than most, he knew what he was up against.

The house servants were terrified but compliant as the now masked man rounded them up and locked them in a store room with orders to make no outcry. Then the murmur of voices and clink of glassware led Harding to the dining room.

No one turned to look. He was practically invisible. They thought he was just another servant awaiting commands as they sat around the rosewood table, six people consuming a meal that might have sustained a peon family for a week.

Don José had not changed since Harding worked for him during a cattle war a few years earlier. A spare, arrogant man in his forties, he was an aristocrat born and bred. His wife was a comely woman with fine, flashing blue eyes. His daughter a nubile slip of a girl whom Don José guarded as zealously as he did his wealth – maybe more. The guests, two men and a woman from a neighbouring *hacienda*, were complaining about the interruption to their normal supplies of mail and goods from the south because of the depredations of the raiders.

Pausing by the ornate servery, Harding tugged his bandanna higher over his nose and stood there listening with a .45 in either hand as the unwitting diners continued their conversation.

The neighbouring rancher lamented the inability of the law to deal with the Benitez menace on this occasion as it had done before. His lady wife expressed a desire to see Juan Manuel Benitez drawn and quartered in the plaza. Don José did not agree. He reminded his guests that he and Juan Manuel Benitez had a working understanding: Juan Manuel Benitez left San Cristóbal alone, and in turn, Don José allowed him to ravage and pillage beyond his borders.

'These human scum are like a force of nature, like flood, fire and famine,' he said. 'One must simply discover how best to deal with them.' He spread smooth hands and added, 'With Juan Manuel Benitez, the most effective method is to live and let live. He lusts for my wealth but fears my strength. I in turn am contemptuous of his excesses but anxious to avoid a costly war with him. So we live and let live and . . .'

He broke of as Cotton Harding stepped into the light of the candelabra. The red bandanna covered his face. His naked six-guns looked the size of cannons in the genteel setting. The neighbour's wife fainted clear away and slumped on to the table.

'Relax!' Harding grated as Don José started to get up. 'Your servants are locked up, and nobody else knows I'm here, so . . .'

'How in the name of the Virgin did you get in here?' Don José Antonio Parra whispered sternly.

'It is not *how* you need to be worried about,'

Harding answered. 'It is *why*.'

His glance went to the richly coloured oil painting depicting the Madonna and Child. He holstered one six-shooter. Keeping the table covered with the other, he went to the painting and took it down. Set in the wall behind it was a steel safe. Harding nodded to a slack-jawed Don José.

'How did you know about that?' Don José demanded, jumping to his feet now. 'You must have been here before. Do I know you, *bandito*?'

'I don't have much time,' Harding stated directly. 'So get busy. I will have it all.'

Don José Antonio Parra looked ill. He always kept a lot of money in his safe, and Cotton Harding knew it. He also knew that few men admired the glint of yellow gold as much as did Don José Antonio Parra, a rich, very ruthless and very greedy man.

'I could shout for help,' Don José threatened angrily. 'My men would come, and you would be dead.'

'But you wouldn't be alive to see it,' Harding replied coldly. 'Señora, better talk some sense into your husband. I will get that thing open over his dead body if I have to.' He hoped it would not come to that.

Harding knew the *señora* to be a sensible, practical woman. She spoke to Parra in low tones. Finally, the *ranchero* nodded grimly, and then went to the safe.

'Very well, you shall have what you desire,' the wealthy ranchero said. 'But you should know you will not get away with this, *gringo*. I shall see you fed to the dogs, and. . . .'

'Just open it!' Harding rapped impatiently. 'Now!'

With a shrug, Don José began working the tumbler. Harding was sweating heavily from the strain and exertion. Unwittingly, he removed sweat from his forehead with a characteristic one-fingered gesture that wasn't lost on the man he was robbing.

'Harding?' Don José breathed. 'I knew that I had seen you before. *Madre*, this is unbelievable. You, of all the *pistoleros* who have worked for me, I believed you to be an honest man.'

'The safe!' Harding snarled, angry to have been identified, angry again because he was forced to do something that went hard against the grain. 'Shut your mouth and get it open.'

As Don José turned back to the safe, the daughter – Delfina – asked breathlessly. 'Is it really you, Señor Harding?'

Disgusted and resigned, Cotton Harding pulled down the red bandanna. They recognized the face but not his expression.

'Sorry,' he said to the young girl. 'I would have come and asked for help if I had thought for one minute that I would get it. Unfortunately, your father is as tight-fisted as he is rich, as everybody knows. . . .'

The safe clicked open and Don José Antonio Parra stepped back.

'You're a dead man, Harding,' he said flatly. 'It will take more than your fast gun to save you. I shall have your life if it is the last thing I do.'

This was no idle threat, Harding knew. Don José

was nothing if not a man of his word. A hard hater and an unforgiving enemy, he never overlooked a slight or forgot a wrong. But nothing he could threaten could measure up to Juan Manuel Benitez.

Every eye followed Harding as he moved to the open safe. It was packed solid with bundles of paper money and little sacks of gold. Harding himself had been paid in gold more than once while hiring his gun to Don José. He began stuffing everything inside his shirt. He hoped nobody would try anything foolish. If they did not believe he would kill, they were sadly mistaken.

Even Don José in his rage was not about to risk his life against a man whose abilities he knew so well. He confined his hostility to words.

'You have sunk far since riding for San Cristóbal, Harding,' he accused, striking a pose at the head of the table as he watched his money vanish inside a dark blue shirt. 'The step down from a *pistolero* to common thief is a great one. What *happened?* Have you lost your nerve for combat? Have you perhaps heard one death rattle too many?'

Cotton Harding said nothing. His shirtfront now bulged with money. He was scraping out a handful of loose gold pieces from the floor of the safe. He needed every centavo.

'*Sí*, I recognize the signs of cowardice,' Don José Antonio Parra continued, speaking to the others now. 'A sad thing to see, is it not? A man who once could hold his head up amongst the bravest *pistoleros* in Mexico, and now he is fearful of death, but without the character to change or become an honest, working man. What you see here is the wreck of a man.'

'Don't overdo it,' Harding said evenly. 'Just remember that if you were more of a man of honour and less of a graspin' greaser who'd sell out his own people to save his skin I could've come to ask you for help instead of takin' it.'

'Of what do you speak, *gringo?*' Don José blustered.

'Juan Manuel Benitez.'

Don José's face closed. He shrugged.

'The doings of this scum have nothing to do with me,' he said calmly.

'That's a lie.' Harding knew this to be a fact.

The sharp look Don José darted at the others told Harding he was afraid of what might be revealed if he went on.

'You have what you came for,' Don José snapped. 'Go on, get out of here!'

But Harding had something more to say, 'They tell me in Hermanas Pozos that you've got a deal with Juan Manuel Benitez. They say that you've agreed not to interfere with *El Azotar*, no matter what they do to the rest of the province, and in return Juan Manuel Benitez doesn't bother you. And seein' as this is the third time he's been through here in the past five years and hasn't set a pony hoof on San Cristóbal soil once, it looks like the stories are true.'

Don José Antonio Parra's face darkened.

'You will pay for that lie,' he spat, 'I am a man of

honour and—'

'Write me a letter about it,' Harding said as he strode to the door. 'I am takin' a horse. I mean to leave quiet and peaceful, but if you raise the alarm, there's a good chance people will die.' A pause. 'Maybe even you. Think about that when I am gone. And the rest of you, think about what I said about the *señor* and Juan Manuel Benitez. Think about it especially when you hear how many innocent people are dyin' in La Tenajo and Santa Rosa, and how much an outfit the size of San Cristóbal could do about it, if it wanted.'

Harding hit the porch at a run and dashed across the huge walled courtyard to the stables. He knew the layout so well that he was astride a long-legged mount and heading for San Cristóbal's wide open spaces before the first gunshots sounded.

'Do not let this man escape!' Don José was shouting now. 'It is Cotton Harding, the *pistolero*!'

Men spilled from the bunkhouses as the racing horseman hammered by. A scatter of shots followed him as he went careening away through the fields of tall corn.

Cotton Harding rode without rest to reach the town at daybreak.

CHAPTER 6

ONLY
GUNSLINGERS
NEED APPLY

The dark-eyed adulteress who shared Brazos Bill's bed lay with the coverlet drawn all the way up to the bridge of her button nose. Her brown eyes were enormous as she stared at Harding over the little hills created by her breasts and feet. The girl seemed embarrassed to be sharing a bedroom with two men, but the American gunmen were not. Between them over the years, Harding and Brazos Bill had probably seen it all. The only difference was that Brazos Bill sampled as he went along while Harding kept temptation at arm's length.

Other than that, there wasn't much difference between the two men. That was either good or bad, depending on your perspective.

61

'All you had to do was ask,' Brazos Bill was saying in his mocking way as he sat up against the ornate headboard. 'Join you at Hermanas Pozos and get chewed up by Juan Manuel Benitez before I even have time to take a drink? No trouble. What are pards for?'

They had never been pards. Both were *gringo* gunfighters who had spent several years in Mexico, whose trails had sometimes crossed, and who on two occasions had found themselves fighting side by side. Each respected the other as a top gun and tough trader, but that wasn't friendship.

'I see you ain't changed any since I last saw you,' Harding grunted and added a nod.

Brazos Bill reached for one of his cigars, unabashed by the situation or his nakedness.

'Neither have you,' he said. 'Still the kind who'll barge in on any man without knockin', like you got some special rights.' He winked as he struck a match. 'A man could get killed that way, you know. . . .'

The girl gave Brazos Bill a nudge beneath the covers and a slight giggle.

'Huh?' he grunted as she whispered to him. 'Oh, yeah, all right.' He grinned around his freshly lit cigar. 'She wants you to turn your back while she gets out of bed. She is kind of naked, you see.'

'Judas Priest!' Cotton Harding sighed impatiently. 'All right, *señorita*.' He turned away. 'Now go on, get!'

Harding realized that he was facing a big bureau mirror as he turned in profile to the bed, and suddenly there she was in the glass, naked as the day she was born and a creamy honey gold from head to toe. Visibility was so good, in fact, that he even noted the mole on her left thigh before she skipped out the door, quite satisfied that modesty had been preserved.

'Where do you get them, Bill?' he asked, turning back. Then he shook his head and added, 'No, don't tell me. I don't want to know. Besides, we got business to discuss. Serious business.'

A cloud of expensive tobacco smoke hung in the still air. Through the haze, Brazos Bill watched his visitor with strange amber eyes that could glow as warm as the sun or turn as cold as a lynx's, depending on this mood. Lean, muscular, hawk-faced and dashing in a dangerous way, Brazos Bill the Texan was probably the deadliest gunman Harding knew, a man who regularly commanded big money to exercise his lethal talents. As far as Harding knew, Brazos Bill had no friends. He was the ultimate loner, self-sufficient and with no known weakness, unless it might be vanity.

He was glad he never had to face him in a gunfight.

'Forget it,' Brazos Bill drawled, swinging his bare feet to the floor. He moved to the window with feline grace.

His severe puckered bullet scars were the only blemishes on a perfect physique. He glanced back over his shoulder with the morning light behind him.

'What beats me,' he said, 'is what made you think

you could come here and talk me into your dumb scheme. I don't get that thinking at all.'

The 'dumb scheme' was Harding's plea to join him to defend Hermanas Pozos against The Scourge when they finally crossed The Nape. Harding had put his request the moment he entered the room, and now he furnished the details. Brazos Bill appeared unimpressed.

'Don't give me that hearts-and-flowers crap, Harding. You say you're doin' all this because of some female? Old keep them-woman-away-from-me Harding. Bullshit! And don't try and switch horses and tell me your heart's bleedin' over a bunch of half-starved Mexicans, either. You see, I know you too well. I know you always look out for number one and don't have any more time for Mexicans than I do. That rules out love and romance and Christian charity, so what have you got left?'

Cotton Harding took the saddlebags slung over his shoulder then tossed them carelessly on the bed, they jingled and bounced a little as they landed.

'This,' he said with confidence.

Brazos Bill looked at the saddlebags before he returned to the bed and undid one of the flaps. His amber eyes widened when he saw the wads of bank notes packed in solidly. He stared at Harding with new interest.

'Hell! How much have you got here? Did you rob a bank or somethin'?' Brazos Bill asked.

'Or somethin'. So now that you know I am offerin' you a payin' job, what's your answer, Bill?'

'You shouldn't have to ask, pard. Count me in.'
Brazos Bill smiled as he answered with a grin.

It seemed that Cotton Harding drew the first easy
breath in the past few days. The big challenges had
been the money and Brazos Bill.

He hoped the rest be as easy.

Somehow, he knew it wouldn't.

Juan Manuel Benitez made his slow, swaggering way
through the plaza of Santa Rosa, second of the three
Twin Lakes towns.

In the big square, now thick with dust, several
hangings were taking place. Juan Manuel Benitez
had called upon the people of Santa Rosa to surrender, and they declined. He warned them that any
man who resisted could expect nothing but death.
Resistance had been weak while *El Azotar*, buoyed up
by their bloody victory at La Tenajo, had proven irre-
sistible. In a short battle, Juan Manuel Benitez lost a
handful of men while the townspeople's casualties
had been at least ten times that amount. They would
be even higher by the time The Scourge hangmen
were finished.

Juan Manuel Benitez paused by a line of carts and
wagons drawn up along the eastern side of the plaza.
There was a variety of vehicles here, from the simple
wooden carts of the villagers to the big prairie
schooners of the American tradesmen.

Sharp smells assailed the outlaw's senses. They
were the familiar scents of his country – animals,
people, beans, chili, fried meat, tortillas, pinion and

cheap liquor. There were also the smells of fire, terror and blood.

Juan Manuel Benitez remembered a better time in his life when he was a young man and the country around him offered all hope. It was a country that was once richly endowed by nature, whether considered from the standpoints of material riches or magnificent scenery. Its forests were extensive, and its mines had scarcely begun to be developed. It was a county of mountain peaks, fruitful valleys and wide plains. It had rivers and lakes by the score, and its canyons were majestic. Its verdant plains swept for unbroken miles to the eastward, covered with thousands of sheep and cattle. At the present time the people of the county were compelled to import much grain, hay, vegetables and other food and forage. It was said that the entire cultivated area of the county did not exceed three thousand acres. In other words, they were forced to depend on others for survival. That was something Juan Manuel Benitez hated.

'Do you remember our last meeting?' Juan Manuel Benitez shouted, snapping back to the here and now. 'DO YOU?'

The people hung their heads and sweated in terror. Like dumb beasts, they accepted the fact that what had befallen them was retribution for the part they played in the three-town defiance of *El Azotar* two years ago. Their 'crime', if you could call it a crime and no one other that the real criminals would, had been to stand against what was happening, and now because they were conditioned to always anticipate the very worst they were seldom rewarded with anything but disappointment.

Juan Manuel Benitez laughed heartily. When a threshing, kicking body was hauled up on a rope from the back of one of the wagons to thud headfirst against the sweeping bough of a cottonwood tree, he laughed even harder.

He stopped by the fountain as his scouts came racing into the plaza. The men had just returned from scouting the country beyond The Nape. It was one of the most fruitful areas of all the land. The valley spread out to a fertile plain, some considerable miles in width and even further in length. Through the plain meandered off-stream of the Rio Grande to where it entered The Nape and the Twin Lakes. To the east, some miles in distance, rose the range of mountains whose tall pinnacles resembled the pipes of an monster organ, while to the west the walls of the table land rose some hundred feet above the level of the valley.

Juan Manuel Benitez's men were pleased to report that, unlike the towns of La Tenajo and Santa Rosa, Hermanas Pozos was showing no signs of preparing a defence.

Benitez smiled from ear to ear. This made him happy.

'From what we see and hear,' said the chief scout, 'they are paralyzed by fear, like the bird who sees the snake.'

'There is nobody at The Nape then?' Juan Manuel

Benitez asked.

'Nobody anywhere except within the town,' one of his scouts was able to tell him. 'And a very frightened town it seems to be.'

The other scouts nodded agreement and there was extra zip and swagger in Juan Manuel Benitez's stride as he walked away – with the skull of his son tucked under his arm. He did not see the strange looks on the scouts' faces in reference to the skull; a good thing for them, he didn't.

'Did I not promise you all of this, Marco?' he crooned. 'Did I not say there would be fire and death and the lakes awash with blood? The days, weeks and years have merely strengthened my passion for revenge. Now it is at hand . . . soon, I shall have it, son . . . soon.'

The rabble pacing several respectful steps behind him exchanged glances. Some regarded their leader as eccentric; others contended that he was as crazy as a loon. But loco or sane, Juan Manuel Benitez was a winner and leader of a massive bandit army. He had the charisma and determination to fight back from the very brink of extinction to again lead a bandit army that could bring entire towns to their knees. Many of The Scourge were already beginning to believe that, with Hermanas Pozos eventually ground out, they would see many more flock to their ranks and enable Juan Manuel Benitez to complete the final phase of his grand plan.

With the three towns crushed, Juan Manuel Benitez planned to ride on the San Cristóbal ranch and wipe it out, leaving not a stone upon stone.

He said that his son had told him to do so in a dream.

Who were they to doubt him?

CHAPTER 7

A QUICK DEATH IS ALWAYS BEST

'Darling? Are you there, darling?' Nina Marie said feebly.

Doctor Hector Colón clutched the patient's feverish hand and told a lie. 'He just left for a moment, *señorita, uno momento*. Sleep now, and when you awake again, he will be with you as before. You want to be rested for him, *sí?*'

Nina Marie was having one of those brief moments of clarity that can come to a fever patient even at the height of the illness. She did not accept the lie, and her thin face looked stricken as she gazed around the room.

'Something has happened to him,' she whispered with a weak voice. 'I know it. He would never stay away from me unless something terrible had happened . . . he loves me so, you see . . . he loves me.'

The medicine man just comforted her without saying anymore until sleep took her again.

'He loves nobody but himself,' Doctor Colón said to Eugenio out on his stoop some time later after finally getting the patient back to sleep. 'If there is a creature more selfish than a *gringo*, it is a *gringo pistolero*. Although Señor Harding is aware that perhaps the *señorita*'s very life depends on him being here at her side, he has gone and I know we shall not see him again. He has gone off to save himself and the woman he professes to love may perish alone . . . along with all of us.'

Eugenio stroked his chin and gazed south over the rooftops towards the twin lakes.

'Perhaps you speak truly,' he murmured, 'perhaps. . . .'

'There is no uncertainty, Eugenio. For is the *pistolero* not gone, leaving us to our doom?' noted the old medicine man.

'Well, he has certainly gone, but maybe he will return,' the young man replied.

'Do you also believe in ghosts, goblins and fairies, young man? Why would the *pistolero* return here now? Our enemies are poised to strike, and soon we shall all be dust. Surely, it would take the bravest of fools to come back now, and Señor Harding is neither brave nor a fool. He is merely a . . . a. . . .' He searched for the exact epithet. 'A *pistolero*!'

'*Sí*,' Eugenio agreed, but he still suspected that

Hermanas Pozos had not seen the last of the *gringo* gunfighter – Cotton Harding.

He was about the only one in town who believed this though.

Then there was Buck 'Little' Mann.

Little Mann, as he was called, was a very different proposition from Brazos Bill, even though they followed the same crimson trade. Small, as his nickname implied, personable and charming in an almost adolescent way, Little Mann could gun down a running jackrabbit at a hundred yards with a six-gun in either hand. He was one of the few men on either side of the Rio Grande who could genuinely boast of surviving a gunfight with Wild Bill Hickok.

Little Mann loved to fight and hated Indians and Mexicans, so when Harding offered him a gunfighting job defending a town against the famed bandit king Juan Manuel Benitez, he could not accept quickly enough.

Next on Harding's shopping list was Jack Olinger – 'Long-haired' Jack as he was better known. Like all the others he was hunting down, this gunman liked to hang his hat in or near Mesilla.

Not surprisingly, Harding located Long-haired Jack at the gambling tables in a smoke-filled dive in the small town of Mesilla. With a cigar in one hand and his black hat tilted to the back of his sleek head, Jack was trimming the suckers like always to avoid working up to a serious confrontation. Harding came straight out with an offer to make big money with the Colt at maximum risk.

'I like the way you put that, Harding,' Long-haired Jack smiled, giving the curvy dancer one final farewell pat on the bottom that almost precipitated the threatened showdown with her man. 'Seemed this indoor life was softening me up anyway. When do we start?'

The answer to that was – not quite yet. Cotton Harding needed more men. He picked up wild and hairy 'Tiger' Sam Sperry and the sombre Tom Bullock, a wanted man in the States, at a cat house in an adjacent town. Then he signed on former Texas Ranger Avery Brennan, and a former Union soldier, Wes Haley, both recovering from wounds taken in a Sierra ambush that occurred several weeks earlier.

Seven skilled and proven gunslingers with no allegiances other than that to their murderous craft and the silver dollar. Men who would not walk one yard to defend a maiden in distress or uphold the honour of Old Glory anymore, but professionals to the bootstraps, each known personally to Cotton Harding and all willing to take the big chances involved in stopping Juan Manuel Benitez, providing the money was right.

Harding went looking for two more, which would bring the total to ten, counting himself. He would rather have ten top gun hands he could rely on than a hundred would-be or second-rate soldiers.

Mesilla was where men like Harding came to spend their blood money and wait for the next job. Bo Fisher, who looked too old and decrepit to ride a horse, much less handle a gun with style and skill, was sharing accommodation with a buxom woman who was delighted with his youthful vigour between the sheets. She gave Harding a fierce calling out when she realized that he had come to take her aged but lively lover away from her.

'*Gringos* with guns!' she screeched. 'You will find them on every street corner, *hombre*. Leave the old man with me so he may die in bed.'

Harding looked her up and down and said, 'And by the looks of you, that wouldn't be too long from now, honey.' Then to Bo, he said, 'I am new at this game of hirin', old man. Likely I should paint a pretty picture of the job, but instead I'm tellin' you there's one hell of a good chance of getting killed out there.'

'I'm too old to die, Harding. Let's go,' Fisher retorted.

Otto Larsen wasn't too old to die, although it was amazing that he was still alive. They called him a crazed killer, and they were right. Harding had heard the tales of his doings. Harding had even fought against Otto in an ugly gun-running feud a year earlier, and he knew him to be as dangerous as a cornered mother bear protecting her cubs. But Otto Larsen was a natural born killer, and that was the kind of man Harding presently needed.

If it was not already too late.

The sense of urgency mounted in Harding as he mustered his band in the breathless hush of early morning. There was no telegraph from Hermanas

Pozos, no way of knowing if the town still existed. In Mesilla, there was little talk of El Azotar. Mexicans accepted the excesses of brigand kings like Juan Manuel Benitez as they did poverty, earthquake and storm. When the subject of The Scourge came up, they might shrug and roll their eyes as if to say, 'what can be done?' Those who knew the reason for Harding's visit were almost unanimous in the opinion that all he would succeed in doing would be to get himself killed. A group of women and friends of his guns for hire gathered to watch Cotton Harding lead them from the shadow-shrouded square. Most were convinced that they were seeing them for the last time.

'I shall always love you!' called one of Little Mann's pretty conquests. 'I shall send flowers when you are buried.'

'Cheerful little thing, ain't she?' Little Mann said ruefully to wild Tiger Sam. 'And to think she was with me when that gypsy told me I would live to be as old as Methuselah.'

'Nobody's that old,' Tiger Sam Sperry said with a crooked, yellow-stained teeth grin.

They were full of energy and enthusiasm for the new adventure as they left the sprawled city behind, but the joking and chatting didn't last long. They soon saw that Harding was going to set a brutal pace.

Sunrise found them far out on the dun plains, nearly a dozen riders startling the birds from their nests in the grass.

*

Juan Manuel Benitez allowed the coins to slide through his thick, callous fingers in a golden shower. Several fell to the floor, but although his lieutenants dived eagerly after them, the leader himself showed no interest. With a sudden sweep of his forearm, he brushed the whole heap of coins to the floor and then tipped over the table. Its edge slammed across the bare foot of the man tied to the bed.

'Chicken scratch!' he said contemptuously as he slapped the prisoner's face. 'Where is the real treasure, pig?' He spat with his request.

There was, of course, no treasure in the town. The gold represented a lifetime's money-grubbing savings to the Santa Rosa storekeeper. If the man had more, he would have surrendered it without hesitation. The Scourge had already murdered his wife and children to impress him with their total seriousness. He had nothing left to live for.

When the storekeeper was dead, Juan Manuel Benitez's fleshy face took on a petulant expression. He walked from the store and then came to a sudden halt.

Santa Rosa was now a landscape of death. Limp figures dangled from hang ropes. In the centre of the square, a dead horse lay bloating in the fierce heat. Flies buzzed and swarmed. The town smelled of death and blood. Raiders wandered through the wreckage, shooting out windows and gunning down dogs. The stench was nauseating.

Santa Rosa was finished. Gone. Any flashes of resistance and grit had been long since eliminated. The thrill was gone, and the dullness reflected in Juan Manuel Benitez's eyes.

'Where is Erasmo?' he shouted, and moments later the narrow-faced man came trotting from the hotel, fitting his big floppy hat to his head. Erasmo Gonzalez was a sharp-eyed sadist whose taste for blood matched the leader's own. Juan Manuel Benitez kept moving through the ruins, forcing Erasmo to trot after him.

'What is it, my master?' the man panted when he drew level.

'Tell me how it was.'

When one man knew another as well as Erasmo knew Juan Manuel Benitez, understanding could often be achieved with a bare minimum of words or even gestures. On this occasion, Erasmo knew exactly what it was that Juan Manuel Benitez wanted to hear.

'We were desperate, my master,' he said, adopting a storyteller's sombre manner. 'The *Federales* and *Rurales* had hounded us for many weeks, and our men were failing with every mile from wounds and from hunger. . . .'

'But what did we believe?' Juan Manuel Benitez broke in.

'We believed that when we reached Twin Lakes and the three towns, there would be bread and meat and shelter for us.'

'But what did we find instead?' Benitez asked.

'Empty lands, Juan Manuel Benitez. No sheep, cattle or grain. We found all the town peons had

retreated to the towns with their food and their families. We found the towns ringed by defenders who
drove us off with their guns while their horsemen
sped off to lead our enemies in on our flanks and
rear. . . .'

It was working. Juan Manuel Benitez's eyes were
no longer dull. Although satiated by blood and lust,
his spirits were now reviving, just as he wanted.

He halted in front of a bullet-scabbed adobe wall
and stared at the smoke-filled sky.

'And what befell us then?' he demanded with a
flash of anger.

'The great Juan Manuel Benitez decided we would
abandon our attempt to force our way into La Tenajo
and Santa Rosa and make one final attempt to
breach the defences of Hermanas Pozos.' Erasmo
paused and then added quickly, 'The only sensible
chance we could take.'

Juan Manuel Benitez moved on again.

'But the gates of Hermanas Pozos were closed
against us,' Juan Manuel Benitez intoned. Clear of
the square now, the two men could see all the way to
the shimmer of blue light on the horizon caused by
sunlight coming off the Twin Lakes. He halted and
turned. 'Is that not so, *amigo*?'

'Too true, too terribly true,' Erasmo agreed. 'And
then, as our weakened men fought valiantly to break
down the defences of that accursed town, the most
evil blow of all was struck, the blow that broke the
mighty Juan Manuel Benitez's fighting heart.'
Another pause. 'Shall I continue?'

Juan Manuel Benitez nodded. He wanted the full dose of medicine today. He was warming up, but was not yet the way he wanted to be.

'The noble Marco,' Erasmo Gonzalez continued, using an adjective for Juan Manuel Benitez's son in death that he certainly never earned in life. 'Riding at the head of his men, so young and tall and filled with life, suddenly, in the time a heart takes to beat once, he was struck from the saddle by a flying bullet, dead in the dust before his father could even reach his side. Oh touching, terrible loss!'

A big crocodile tear ran down Juan Manuel Benitez's swarthy cheek. This great affection for his son had only materialized after the young man's death. Alive, Marco Juan Manuel Benitez had been regarded by his father as a rebellious, self-seeking, disobedient and unreliable little swine who was going to require enormous tutoring and discipline to turn him into a worthy successor. But dead, Marco had suddenly assumed all the virtues his father held dear. In Juan Manuel Benitez's mind, if in nobody else's, Marco had become a saint of the owlhoot and an inspiration for murderous excesses.

The two men went to Juan Manuel Benitez's quarters, where the yellowing skull of Marco sat on a littered desk, grinning in the shadowed gloom.

'What does my son tell me, Erasmo?' the bandit king asked.

Erasmo had to think fast at times like this. He had to guess what Juan Manuel Benitez wanted to hear, and guessing wrong could be dangerous.

'Er ... ahh ... Marco says that ... that we have given Hermanas Pozos enough time to suffer every possible agony of fear, and that now we should ride north and ... er, set about the real business of our raid, the total destruction of the third town?'

There was a rising inflection on that final word, for Erasmo wanted to know if he had guessed right, or if he should start ducking.

He began sweating in relief as Juan Manuel Benitez picked up the skull and nodded his shaggy head.

'And my son, as always, is right,' he said in a soft voice. 'Erasmo,' he smiled, 'give orders to our leaders to muster their men. I want every man in his saddle and ready to ride within the hour.'

It was a relieved Erasmo Gonzalez who trotted out into the punishing sunshine and began to shout orders.

CHAPTER 8

KILLERS OR SAVIOURS?

'Howdy, everyone!' Brazos Bill called as they clattered over the rickety wooden bridge that led into the town. 'We have come to save your sorry asses, so how about a cheer or two?'

Below the bridge, the women and children of the town straightened from their washing chores. Although the shadow of disaster had hung over Hermanas Pozos ever since Juan Manuel Benitez's forces roared into La Tenajo many days ago, life continued much as it had always done. There were still meals to prepare, washing to be done, and babies to tend. Today was wash day, and the banks of the river were littered with piles of clothing waiting to be pounded clean.

Not one of the townspeople cheered. They had no

idea who these men might be, only that they were not *El Azotar*, which was a huge relief. Then somebody recognized the tall, lean figure of Harding amongst the dangerous looking *gringo*s. This started them murmuring among themselves.

'Stupid fools,' Brazos Bill sneered as his beautiful tan horse careered off the bridge. 'I have seen smarter beeves in my time, I swear I have. Ignorant fools.'

'Ungrateful fools, is more like it,' countered the beastly Tiger Sam Sperry. 'They play good guitar and the long-haired ones ain't bad in bed.'

'Seems like they are not the only stupid ones,' Brazos Bill replied in his mocking, superior way.

'And that means?' Tiger Sam asked with impertinence.

Brazos Bill turned to Harding and said, 'Hey, I thought you said that this dump was in a sweat about Juan Manuel Benitez. Where are the lookouts?'

Cotton Harding looked around. There were no lookouts to be seen, no sign of armed men of the town on any of the hot and dusty streets. Even before he left the town, he had sensed that Hermanas Pozos was slipping into a state of apathetic shock. It was apparent at a glance that its slide had become complete during his absence.

If this was not a town without any backbone left, then he had yet to see one. It was a town already beaten by cowardice and fear.

'If they could watch out for themselves, I wouldn't have needed you fellas,' he replied.

The cavalcade clattered past the first squat adobes. Skinny men, slatternly women and half naked kids filled doorways to watch them pass. A gaunt ribbed hound came yapping out from a gateway to nip at the heels of Wes Haley's horse. It yipped as Wes hauled out his six-gun and drove a bullet between its legs.

'Save the gunpowder till later, Wes!' Harding called back. 'Likely you will need all you can get then, and then some.'

The crash of the shot drew people into the streets. They watched with open mouths as the riders approached the square. Although isolated and unsophisticated, the peasants of Hermanas Pozos could recognize *gringo* gunfighters at a glance and were taken aback to see ten of the breed coming into town with Cotton Harding.

'You sure you want to save this sorry lot, Harding?' called Otto Larsen, scratching his ear with his gun muzzle as he gazed back over the people of the town. 'I mean to say is . . . why?'

'Don't you know?' Brazos Bill grinned, as they entered the square. 'You mean to save Hermanas Pozos from the torch so you can convert it into a graveyard. Hell, all you would have to do would be liven it up first . . . Christ almighty, this is a pitiful place!'

Some of the men laughed because they were amused, others because they were a little in awe of Brazos Bill and thought it best to go along with whatever he did or said. A few, like the always sombre Tom Bullock, gaunt-faced Avery Brennan and Bo Fisher, paid very little, if any, attention. These men were not here for the fun of it all, but to fight; and the sooner the fighting started, the better.

Harding could no longer feign nonchalance as he brought the tiny tin-roofed hospital into his sight. He kicked his horse into a lope and left his gunmen staring after him curiously.

'As I recall, Harding wasn't always this mysterious,' opined Long-haired Jack Olinger the gambler gunman with the pencil thin moustache. 'Wonder what has got into him?'

'He would have his reasons,' Buck 'Little' Mann said, tipping his hat to a couple of sloe-eyed *señoritas*. 'Harding never did nothin' without a good reason.'

'And you can take the word of a died-in-the-wool hero worshipper for that,' Brazos Bill said loudly.

'Sure, I admire Cotton Harding,' Buck 'Little' Mann said readily. 'Who do you admire? Apart from yourself, that is?'

Brazos Bill lifted a lazy eyebrow in Little Mann's direction. In experience, he was way ahead of the youthful gunfighter. Despite his big reputation, earned honestly during his bloody soldier-of-fortune years south of the border, he could not be certain that he was better than this baby-faced man of the Colts. Since Little Mann had splashed across the Rio Grande just half a mile ahead of a posse of Texas Rangers a year ago, he had shown himself to be a gun-packer to take very seriously.

Men were gathering on the porch of Flo's cantina as the horsemen headed unerringly in its direction.

'Is it true,' asked a bright-eyed young Mexican, 'that you have come here with Señor Harding?'

'What's it to you, *amigo*?' growled Bo Fisher, reining in his horse at the rail.

Eugenio smiled hopefully.

'It is important, *señor*,' he replied with a slight smile, 'for if you are indeed friends of Señor Harding's, it means you may have come to help us and our town.'

'Nobody comes to help us, Eugenio,' the mayor said in a funereal voice.

He wore black as though in readiness for his own death. Fisher thought it was appropriate, but cowardly nonetheless.

The older Bo Fisher swung down with a lithe grace that belied his years.

'Tie up my horse,' he said to the mayor. 'Here's a centavo.'

It was a deliberate insult. It was obvious that the mayor was a man of some importance, just as it was plain as day that Fisher knew it. This mean old gunman, like Brazos Bill and Otto Larsen, was a hater of Mexicans. Hatred kept him going and he had plenty to go around.

As the mayor flushed in anger, Eugenio stepped forward to take the reins and wrap them securely around the hitch rail.

Eugenio smiled up at the glowering Fisher and asked, 'Have you come to fight Juan Manuel Benitez, *señor*?'

'Depends,' Bo Fisher said around a wad of tobacco

in his jaw.

'On what, *señor*?' the mayor asked almost rudely.

'On whether we can whip The Scourge without helpin' you yeller-bellied fools or not,' came the corresponding insulting reply.

Across the square at Doc Colón's, Cotton Harding could not stop smiling. Nina Marie Romero was still alive. Colón claimed she hadn't made much progress and was still to be described as critical – dying – but Harding could see she had not slipped any further away either. He was relieved.

Even though she slept now and her face was the colour of marble in contrast to the damp darkness of her hair, he sensed that she knew he was there. He could feel it in her fingers as he lifted them to his lips.

The old Mexican doctor looked on and marvelled that a man of such a brutal calling could care for another person the way Harding apparently did for this woman.

'It's cool in here,' Harding remarked with some pleasure. 'Have you been keepin' your roof watered?'

Doctor Hector Colón nodded. He had worn his young helper out, insisting that he climb up to the roof with pails of water every day.

'Good man . . . doc. . . .'

Harding paused for a moment and then groped inside his shirt to produce a small sack of gold dust, which he dumped onto the night table. 'There's more where that come from, old man. Keep up the good work.'

Doc Colón quickly snatched the sack from the table.

'Should I not perhaps return this to San Cristóbal, Señor Harding?' he asked softly.

'Huh?' Harding said.

'Señor,' the doctor said, 'it is no secret what you did. You are now a *bandito*... but I suppose you know this?'

Harding grinned. Since thundering away from San Cristóbal with his saddle-bags filled with money, he had not given Don José another thought.

Now he was a wanted man. Well, it did not seem like such a big thing. Not under the circumstances. But somehow it was.

He was sober as he got up from the bedside chair. They left Nina Marie Romero with the plump nurse and went to the ante room, where a Mexican with a bloodied arm was waiting to see the doctor.

'What is the latest on Juan Manuel Benitez?' Harding enquired.

'Ask this man,' Colón replied, sitting at the Mexican's side to unravel the grimy bandage from his arm. 'He was wounded in the fighting at Santa Rosa and just arrived here in need of my services.'

Harding eyed the Mexican man as he took out tobacco and papers.

'How bad is it?' he asked tentatively.

The medicine man shrugged. 'So bad there is nothing to be said, *señor.*'

'Are *El Azotar* still in Santa Rosa?'

'*Sí*, I mean, they were when I left yesterday,' the man replied without hesitation.

'Do you know anything of their plans?' Harding asked, knowing the man knew what he probably knew anyway.

'Only that it is said they will come here.' The Mexican winced as Doc Colón probed at his arm. 'A friend who died at Santa Rosa told me he saw Juan Manuel Benitez talking with this skull. He told the skull he would destroy Hermanas Pozos.'

With a cigarette going, Cotton Harding went outside to find the skinny boy. He was being very generous with what was left of Don José Antonio Parra's money.

'*Muchas gracias*, Señor Harding. I do good job keeping the roof wet, no?'

'Just keep doin' it, kid. No matter what happens here, you just keep in mind that what you and Doc Colón are doin' is the most important job in the world.'

The young man nodded and stared across the plaza at the line of big horses outside the cantina. Only Avery Brennan, the brooding teetotaller, was in sight. He was standing with one dusty boot on the bench, cleaning his pistol.

'These are your *amigos*, Señor Harding?' Eugenio asked.

'In a way, I guess you could say that,' he responded simply.

'Are they also outlaws like you?' Eugenio asked bluntly.

88

It was going to take some getting used to the idea that he was a wanted man. Gunfighting was far more noble than being a thief.

'No,' he replied dryly, 'they are just killers.'

The young man looked up and added, 'As you are, *señor?*'

'Yeah, all killers, kid. A bunch of butchers, you might even say.'

'Is strange . . .' the boy began and then fell silent.

'What is? C'mon, don't leave somethin' half said, kid.'

'Well, is strange that the *señorita* within should . . .' the boy stopped before completing the sentence.

Again the young man stopped in embarrassment, but Harding got the drift.

'That she should get tied up with an outlaw and a killer like me?' Harding finished for him, going down the steps. 'Sure, that's hard to figure and no mistake.' He paused. 'But you don't have to fret about that, kid. You just take care of keeping that roof cool, and go on doin' it even if the town is full of Juan Manuel Benitez's men tryin' to kill you. You just keep that damn roof wet and watch out for the *señorita.* Got it?'

'*Sí,* Señor Harding, of course.'

The sun struck like a hammerhead across Harding's shoulders as he headed for the cantina. Looking down at his hand, it was as if he could still feel Nina Marie Romero's touch. It made him feel stronger than he had in a long time.

He would need that strength and more.

CHAPTER 9

LET FATE DECIDE

Don José Antonio Parra raised his head as his foreman approached. It was his habit to work on his books in the main courtyard by the fountain. Accounting was a task he would normally enjoy. The rows and rows of neat figures told him how much richer he was becoming and suggested ways to cut costs and increase profits. It was an exercise that gave more pleasure than drinking good wine or making love. But all pleasure was dimmed these days, by the more or less public humiliation of a theft from his home.

The foreman, a man named Jorge Morales, brought a good report. All the grain was in, and the peons were ready for other work.

'Shear the sheep,' Don José ordered.

Jorge Morales nodded obediently and left. The

Don chewed on his pen and then set it aside. He was pouring wine from a clay jug as his daughter Delfina appeared.

She was the only person on San Cristóbal who dared interrupt this way; she was, after all, the apple of his eye, his pride and joy.

Father and daughter were still together in the courtyard some time later when Gregorio arrived. The tall, thin *vaquero* had been absent for a few days, searching for a lead on Cotton Harding, and he had finally dug up some news.

Harding, Gregorio announced, was reported to be in Hermanas Pozos.

Don José Antonio's elation at the news was just as quickly quenched.

'Hermanas Pozos?' he asked, 'now?'

Both Gregorio and his daughter knew what he meant. Of all the places on the great plain where someone might go of his own free will at the moment, Hermanas Pozos would have to be on the bottom of any such list.

Even as Gregorio nodded, Don José was recalling the way Harding had spoken of Hermanas Pozos and Juan Manuel Benitez on the night of the robbery.

'What is his interest in that rat-hole of a town?' he wanted to know.

'Harding has a woman in Hermanas Pozos, Don José,' Gregorio said. 'I am told she suffers from the fever. I am also told that when Harding returned to the town, he was not alone. He brought with him a band of *pistoleros* like himself.'

Staring at his man, Don José massaged his temple as he tried to understand.

'Do you have orders, Don José?' Gregorio asked meekly.

Don José Antonio Parra deliberated. Apart from alerting the law and having wanted papers posted on Harding, he had sent his men in search of Harding. His intention had been to alert the law if his men found Harding, but there were no soldiers near Hermanas Pozos. Juan Manuel Benitez was raging through the region at full strength. Parra had no intention of buying into that, no matter how badly he might want Harding's head. Suddenly, he saw that there was no real need for him to interfere anyway – for didn't everyone know that Hermanas Pozos was doomed?

The rich man began to smile from ear to ear. He was content to sit back and let fate get rid of Cotton Harding for him once and for all.

The narrow strip of rock which separated Lake Gurule from Lake Griego was aptly named. The Nape was long and thin, several hundred yards long by between twenty and fifty yards in width. The trail, worn smooth by generations of travellers, was unprotected by rocks or trees. In wintertime, it was buffeted by the winds that blew strongly across the Twin Lakes, usually from west to east.

There was no wind today. The hot air was breathless, and the wide lakes lay beneath a washed-out blue-hued sky, still as mill ponds. A solitary bird winged low across the empty trail and glided down to the water's edge. Far out across Lake Gurule, two row boats trailed nets in the water.

The northern approach to The Nape was through a crescent of marshland about three hundred yards wide. There was a knoll at the left horn of the marsh and another smaller one across to the right. Wes Haley was immediately reminded of Round Top and Little Round Top on the bloody fields of Gettysburg.

The whole scene reminded Brazos Bill of a bad dream.

'This is where you want us to dig in?' he questioned Harding. 'Tell me you are jokin' with us, having a little fun. . . .'

'I don't reckon you are as dumb as you look, Bill,' Harding grinned. 'A man with half an eye can see this is the only place to set up.'

The gunfighters sat on their saddles, staring out over The Nape and the blue lakes. This was rugged, heat-stricken country. There was farming all over this country and most of it was carried on by primitive methods, but the results obtained even with these often produced wonderful bushels of wheat. With a proper water system from the lakes, it could furnish sufficient water to irrigate all of the land available for agriculture. The locals did not use fertilizer, nor was any needed, as the sediment in the water used in the irrigation answered the purposes of the manufactured articles on the worn-out lands. Harding had been doing his research as he had been planning on settling down, becoming a farmer and living the rest of his life in peace with Nina Marie Romero.

All that had changed.

Although the marsh looked rough and uncom-fortable, it at least provided some cover. That was more than could be said of either The Nape or the landscape immediately at their backs.

'Harding's right,' Haley opined. 'This is where a soldier would settle in, Brazos.'

'So, we are the army now, are we?' Brazos Bill challenged.

He liked to needle, but the truth was that his heart wasn't in it at the moment. The gunfighter had other things on his mind. He kept glancing across at Harding as his companions dismounted to inspect the battleground at close quarters. Brazos Bill expected the worst of everybody and was seldom dis-appointed, but at the moment, Harding had him a little perplexed.

'We will hide the horses over yonder behind the big knoll,' Harding stated.

'Round Top,' Little Mann corrected.

'All right,' Harding conceded. 'Buck, you and Sam and Jack take the mounts across. The rest of you come with me, and we will pick out our positions. All but you, Otto. I want you to cross The Nape and scout around some. I don't have to tell you what you are lookin' for, do I?'

Otto Larsen shook his head in response.

'Ten thousand dirty *banditos*, ain't it?' he asked with a straight face.

'Somethin' like that,' Harding replied, and as Otto trotted off towards The Nape, he led the way to the marsh.

The trail from The Nape had been built up with rocks and stood several feet above the surrounding marsh. Here and there, stands of coarse brushes stood four or five feet high. A flycatcher screeched in annoyance at the interruption and flew off towards Little Round Top.

It was late afternoon, but still punishingly hot. Even so, there was little complaining. These were tough, hard men, all accustomed to rugged conditions and the extremes of weather and human behaviour.

'There is my spot,' said Brennan, indicating a small nest of rocks close by the elevated trail. 'I can snuggle down in there and pick 'em off like quail.'

'If they get this far,' said Tom Bullock, looking at Cotton Harding. 'We don't intend on letting them through, do we, Harding?'

'Not if we can help it,' Harding said and pointed towards The Nape where Otto Larsen was now just a dot in the distance. 'There isn't much cover worth a damn out there for anybody comin' off The Nape, so hot-shot marksmen like us shouldn't have much trouble pickin' 'em off.'

'Sounds simple when you say it quick,' Brennan said in his grating way.

'That is how our clients always say it, Brennan,' Brazos Bill said. 'Ain't that right, Harding?'

Harding was still not used to the new role that circumstances had forced upon him. Like the others, he had always worked for a money man who hired others to be brave on his behalf. In general, gunmen looked down on clients, as Brazos Bill knew only too well. Harding was starting to find the Texan's manner just a little irritating.

'Whatever you say,' he said indifferently.

Brazos Bill stooped to grab a pebble which he shied at the trail.

'Yes, sir, the client will always tell you how easy the job of work is, how the joker you are bein' sent after is half blind with one foot in boot hill – and he turns out to be Wild Bill or somebody havin' a fast day. That is a client's natural style. If he tells you the truth, he is afraid you won't take the job.'

'Has anybody heard me say this was goin' to be an easy job?' Harding frowned.

'Course not,' Bo Fisher said quickly. 'You told us we would be up against The Scourge, and there ain't no way a man can think that is goin' to be anything except close to impossible.'

'Well, you bein' old as dirt, you should know,' Brazos Bill replied. 'But I reckon I should remind you jokers that if that son of a greaser bitch does come this way like they figure, then every mother's son of us is goin' to earn his money or die trying, that much is a fact.'

'We are wastin' time,' Cotton Harding said brusquely. 'If Juan Manuel Benitez comes, he could come awful fast, and I want every man settled in with his guns and ammunition handy. We have lots to do, let's get busy.'

It took them an hour to select and prepare their

positions. Rocks were shifted and formed into barricades. Ammunition boxes were stashed carefully in safe places. Six-guns, rifles and shotguns were all checked and re-checked by men who fully appreciated their importance.

And tension began to mount. It could almost be felt in the air.

Harding could feel it as he took a stroll around the crescent with his Winchester in the crook of his arm. Although the men smoked and joked and displayed overt nonchalance in a dozen or so different ways, he knew they were just a little edgy. It showed in the way they glanced frequently down the gun barrel over The Nape, in the number of cigarettes and cigars they got through, even in their talkativeness.

But mostly he was aware of it through the feeling in his own body. He believed that all good guns felt that way, that it was only the second-raters or the fools who weren't scared when they put their lives on the line.

The odds against them were going to be heavy. Certainly, they had the advantage of terrain, and they were all top gun hands, but estimates of Scourge strength ranged between a hundred and three hundred men. They might be scum, scoundrels and killers, but The Scourge were fighting men, as the towns of Santa Rosa and La Tenajo had already found out. He propped one foot on a rock and stared south. A faint smoke haze clung to the horizon. He had heard conflicting reports on the fate of Santa Rosa, but it seemed certain that it, like

La Tenajo, had suffered brutally at the hands of the raiders.

He felt strangely relaxed as he smoked a good cigarette and watched the sun slide down the sky. The uncertainty and the hustle were now behind him. He had got his money and his gunmen. He had returned before Juan Manuel Benitez made his move on Hermanas Pozos. True, the dangerous part of it all lay ahead, but that was preferable to not knowing if Juan Manuel Benitez was putting Hermanas Pozos to the torch while he was busy elsewhere, or to finding that Nina Marie Romero had slipped away.

His face softened. It had been love at first sight when he met her. He hadn't trusted the emotion at first, but she had changed all that. Nina Marie Romero had convinced this gun-packing adventurer that there could be more to life than riding around Mexico shooting people and getting shot at, and Cotton Harding had surrendered with remarkable speed and ease when she finally came south to take him back.

He never wanted to be parted from her now, but that was something he felt he should not consider too closely.

Whenever a gunfighter plied his trade, there was a good chance he wouldn't survive. Despite the confident attitude he adopted for the benefit of the men, Harding knew deep down inside that this was shaping up as the most dangerous job he had attempted since first buckling on the six-shooters.

Ten men against a so-called army of crazed

Mexican bandits were chilling odds. With more time and a hell of a lot more money, he might have recruited more men. But that was just his dreaming. Ten men versus The Scourge was the reality of this situation, and he was more than satisfied with the men he had been able to muster.

Harding half-smiled to himself. As a gunfighter himself, he knew the breed only too well. What they would never do for love, loyalty, lust or any of the more conventional reasons that drove men to achievement, the average *gringo* gun-packer could always be relied upon to do for gold.

'Harding!'

The shout drifted up to him from Wes Haley's rock nest by the trail. Haley pointed southwards, and looking in that direction, Harding sighted the horse-man riding into The Nape.

He used his field glasses to identify Otto Larsen. He was riding fast but raising little dust on the hard-packed surface of The Nape.

Harding trained the glasses on the horizon. The smoke was still there, but it was mixed with slow rising dust from the plains.

'Everybody in position!' he shouted, heading swiftly back towards the trail as Otto hammered swiftly closer. 'Otto ain't usin' up a horse on a hot day like that for no reason.'

His prediction proved sound. Otto had been about five miles south of The Nape when he sighted The Scourge's advance scouts heading up the Santa Rosa trail. He only delayed long enough to see the full force of riders quit the scarred and blackened town before heading back to report.

'How many do you figure?' Cotton Harding wanted to know.

'Too many,' was the cryptic reply.

Harding's smile was crooked as he looked up at the cold-eyed killer.

'Why then, that is just how we like it, ain't it?'

It was chilling to hear Otto's laughter. It wasn't quite right somehow. It was the kind of laugh a man might hear late at night when passing the asylum.

'You bet your damn life it is,' Otto hooted as he spurred towards Round Top to get rid of his horse.

He waved his Stetson as he stormed past his companions' positions.

'It is going to be a high old time tonight, amigos. There is damn well millions of the bastards.'

Some of the gunfighters began to cheer. Others, like Harding himself, showed little to no emotion at all.

They would not survive. He knew it and they knew. They were dead men; he was a dead man. It seemed strange to hear men cheering their own deaths, but maybe Harding understood. Gunfighting was like anything else in life. A man never figured he would be the one to run out of luck.

It was always going to be the next guy.

CHAPTER 10

THE NAKED SKULL

A horse whinnied ahead as the bandit king Juan Manuel Benitez rode onto The Nape. He set the skull on the saddle pommel, facing forwards. Erasmo Gonzalez flipped a pebble into the gentle, lapping waters of Lake Griego. It splashed. Juan Manuel Benitez's bodyguards looked sharply in the direction of the sound, proving that they were fully alert, which was nothing if not reassuring to the leader of *El Azotar*.

Juan Manuel Benitez drew his sword. Although he rarely got close enough to carry it this way when on the march. At such times, he imagined himself to be a great general en route to Mexico City to accept the government's surrender. His dream never went past the bloody slaughter of the enemy, for when it came down to the nugget of things, Juan Manuel Benitez

101

had interest only in the power to live exactly as he pleased and to kill everybody who tried to stop him.

The cavalcade stretching ahead resembled a genuine army on the march, a victorious army. Horses were laden with plunder and the men rode in the triumphant, casual manner of winners. Bottles winked in the late afternoon sunlight, and not everybody was steady in the saddle. A one-eyed rogue riding a thoroughbred mare played a penny whistle while a companion rattled out a martial beat on a stolen kettle drum.

Juan Manuel Benitez stood in his stirrups to look ahead. His five chief scouts were travelling along The Nape at a lope. Juan Manuel Benitez insisted on keeping alert, even though it seemed certain that Hermanas Pozos would prove no more of a problem than La Tenajo and Santa Rosa.

Juan Manuel Benitez's face wreathed with a reflective smile. As was the case in all well-planned campaigns, the greatest pleasure had been left until last. Juan Manuel Benitez had been hard on La Tenajo and Santa Rosa, very hard. But in Hermanas Pozos, he would demonstrate just how hard his wrath could really be.

When he left Hermanas Pozos, the town would be no more and no less than an open grave, a vast pit of despair.

He was sure that his son smiled at the prospect.

A tall, lean rider galloped up to pass Juan Manuel Benitez, tipping his *sombrero* respectfully as he went by. Juan Manuel Benitez had known the man from

San Cristóbal for several years, but this was the first time he had ridden with them. Jorge Morales, Don José's foreman, had met up with him at Santa Rosa and asked to ride with the army for a spell as an 'observer', on José Antonio Parra's behalf. Juan Manuel Benitez only half-trusted Parra and therefore didn't trust this man at all.

He beckoned Erasmo.

'Why do you believe this man is with us?' he asked.

'He tells me that Parra wants to find the *gringo*, Harding, and believes he might be in Hermanas Pozos,' Erasmo replied.

'Harding. . . ?'

'The *pistolero* who robbed Parra last week, leader,' Erasmo Gonzalez dutifully answered.

'Oh, *sí* . . . Harding.'

Juan Manuel Benitez was still watching Morales' back. The killer had many enemies and many allies. He did not trust either and believed that only by constant suspicion had it been possible for him to survive so long. Finally, he put thoughts of Morales and Parra to one side and returned his full attention to the present.

'We can reach the town at dusk,' he announced after doing some calculating. 'It should be ours within the hour.'

'Perhaps even sooner, Juan Manuel Benitez. Our scouts say that Hermanas Pozos has no spirit left. Once La Tenajo fell and Santa Rosa was under attack, the people of Hermanas Pozos merely sat down to await their fate.'

103

'Ha, cowards, all of them!'

'They shall soon be dead cowards,' said Erasmo, who knew what his master wanted to hear.

Juan Manuel Benitez was nodding agreement when he realized that the vanguard had halted partway across The Nape.

'Halt!' he shouted, lifting his sword.

The cause of the hold-up was plain to Juan Manuel Benitez as he closed on the lead riders. Beyond them, the scouts had stopped dead. Then one scout broke away from the group and came spurring back, beating his horse along with his hat.

'So?' Juan Manuel Benitez shouted impatiently. 'What is it? Why are we stopped?'

The scout drew his horse to a tail-dragging halt and threw a sloppy salute towards Juan Manuel Benitez.

'There is a man up there,' the scout reported. 'A *gringo*. . . .'

The leader of The Scourge narrowed his eyes as he stared ahead. The trail dipped slightly at the end of The Nape and he could see nothing.

'Who is this *gringo*?' Juan Manuel Benitez demanded.

'Harding.'

'Harding?' Erasmo called, riding up. 'Did you say Harding?'

'This is what he calls himself,' the scout replied. 'He tells us that we are not permitted to pass.'

Juan Manuel Benitez's stare grew leaner and more intense.

'What? One man says this to... to us? Is he *loco*?'

'He does not look loco,' the scout answered, glancing back. 'It seems that he is very serious. He says that if we try to pass beyond The Nape, we shall die.'

Juan Manuel Benitez massaged the back of his neck. Behind him, the men were growing restless. His horse stamped on the hard earth, and Erasmo was looking at him with raised eyebrows.

'This then is the same *gringo* who robbed Señor Parra?' Juan Manuel Benitez said after a pause.

'It would seem so, leader,' Erasmo said. 'Harding, the *pistolero*.'

Frowning, Juan Manuel Benitez began stroking the skull on his saddle. *Pistoleros* were too much like Juan Manuel Benitez himself. They, too, were deadly and sometimes moved to mindless violence. But for all of that it would surely be a cold day in Hell before the full force of Juan Manuel Benitez the Bold could be turned back or even hindered by a solitary *gringo pistolero*.

'Kill him,' he ordered simply. 'Kill him at once and let us be on our way.'

'Consider it done, great leader,' said the scout, and swinging his horse, he rode back to his companions and passed on the orders.

The scouts lifted their guns and rode forward.

'Are we ready?' Cotton Harding called out softly.

'Ready!' they answered in unison – Brazos Bill invisible with his repeater Winchester, Little Mann champing at the bit for action. Long-haired Jack

105

lounging gracefully behind his carefully built rock barricade with an unlit cigar, Tiger Sam and Tom Bullock close together near Round Top, with Brennan, Haley, Fisher and Larsen all on the far side of the trail.

Harding stood by the trail, close to Wes Haley's rock nest, with his rifle slanted across his hips and his narrowed eyes following the oncoming horsemen's every step.

Now, Harding's mind shouted.

'Stop!' he barked at the top of his lungs.

The horsemen did not even slow down a bit. They were well within rifle range now, but Harding allowed them to draw closer. There wasn't one in the bunch that didn't look dirty and depraved. They were well named, he laughed to himself. Scourge. But not to be taken lightly. They had notched up a string of victories and radiated the victor's confidence.

One hundred or so yards separated them.

Harding lifted his rifle. No need to shoulder the weapon at this range; he knew what he could do.

'Last chance, Scourge!' he called out. 'Turn back or die!'

They could still only see one man. They kept on coming towards the town – towards Harding. Harding stroked the trigger, and a raider threw up his arms with a cry and rolled off the back of his horse.

Instantly the scouts raised their weapons, nevertheless before they could get off a shot, the marsh came alive with a roaring volley of gunfire.

A hard-hit horse went staggering off the trail. As the rider lifted himself in the stirrups to jump clear, he was hit in the shoulder and stomach areas simultaneously.

Harding kept working the action of his Winchester until bullets began zinging around him. Then he ducked low beneath the shoulder of the built-up trail. Resting the gun barrel on a rock, he continued to lay down gunfire.

The sound was deafening with more than a dozen guns bellowing hot lead.

Two of Juan Manuel Benitez's scouts broke away and came heeling along the trail, each firing as fast as they could.

Excited Buck 'Little' Mann suddenly sprang to his feet and cut loose with his double-barrelled shotgun. Riding into a hail of grey whistlers, one scout sagged in the saddle while his companion went down, horse and all, plunging into a headlong slide that carried both off the lip of the trail.

The wounded man kept charging. His revolver churned, and Little Mann yipped and ducked for cover as the slug bounced off the stock of his shotgun and furrowed his forearm.

Harding's bunch didn't know this man was one of Juan Manuel Benitez's most effective fighters, but they had already assessed him as a formidable opponent.

As Harding lifted his head, two slugs bit the trail near by, spraying him with dirt and rock fragments.

'Get that son of a b. . . !' he roared but unable to finish his words as the gunfire's roar overshadowed them. 'He will be on top of me in a second!'

Gun thunder answered, and up along the trail, the deadly scout got off another few shots at Buck's position, standing in his stirrups to get a better angle.

Then his horse had its legs cut from under it.

The Mexican yelled as he was catapulted forward. He landed awfully hard and dust from the ground rose.

The horse struggled to rise, failed and fell over sideways.

The scout was already up.

The sun glinted on metal, and smoke blossomed darkly before him as he hauled and fired his second belt gun. His defiance drew another volley of gunfire from the marsh, but the gunfighters were triggering at the two scouts who were coming hammering up behind their companion now. These men were Juan Manuel Benitez's elite and were living up to their reputations.

The man on foot was struck again, and his nerve finally showed signs of cracking as he slewed aside and started to run for shelter behind a horse.

The scout fired two quick shots across his body as he ran, but he was running out of luck. Harding saw the panic in the man's face in the split second before a bullet knocked him off his feet.

Harding fired at a rider who jerked erect in the saddle, and then was driven sideways by fire from Otto Larsen and Bo Fisher. The next moment, the horse stumbled to its knees with bloody froth in its nostrils.

Action blurred from there. The scout on foot was trying to seize hold of the remaining horse while its rider continued working a Winchester repeater with noisy effect.

Brazos Bill was standing and pouring in the fire with his Colts.

Little Mann got up with the shotgun, and it thundered like a cannon as it blew the rider out of the saddle.

The gritty scout on foot grabbed the horse's dangling reins and tried to get his boot into stirrup iron.

It seemed that a dozen bullets struck him at once.

The scout doubled up like a closing jackknife, wrapping his arms tightly around his stomach. One leg failed, and he started to go over.

Brazos Bill took careful aim and drilled the scout through the head.

CHAPTER 11

DEATH MARSH

'It ain't nothin', Harding,' insisted Buck 'Little' Mann sheepishly, eager to pick up his shotgun again. 'My old pa used to hurt me more than that with just a switch.'

'Shut up and hold still,' Cotton Harding snapped perhaps too harshly. 'And next time you jump like a damn fool cowboy, I will shoot you myself.'

Chastened although still excited, Buck sat quietly while Avery Brennan bandaged his arm with a strip of torn shirt.

On either side of the trail, sharp eyes watched the outlaws as they came slowly along The Nape in a dark, menacing mass.

'Looks like they are coming all the way!' Brazos Bill called from his rock nest.

'Why shouldn't they?' Harding muttered to Brennan and Mann. 'By now, they would have

110

figured roughly how many of us there are, which means the odds favour them about twenty or so to one.'

'You figure there is almost two hundred or more of them bastards, Cotton?' Little Mann asked.

'Sounds like a fairly accurate guess to me.'

'Oh my lord!'

Brennan put the finishing touches on the bandage and then scooped up his rifle.

'Now you do like Harding says, Buck,' he said gravely. 'Don't be a cowboy.'

Little Mann grinned disarmingly.

'But I am the reckless type, pardner. A tiger can't change its stripes, you know what I mean. What if somebody told you to start actin' like you enjoyed life, Brennan... you would probably haul off and hit them in the face and likely die iffen you did. And you, Harding, you would be the same if you had to stop being crazy, now wouldn't you?'

'Crazy?' Harding dragged his eyes away from the enemy. 'Who's crazy?'

'Harding,' Little Mann said pleasingly, reasonably, 'you have made yourself an outlaw and spent a fortune to try and defend a town that can't be defended from a Scourge army that can't be stopped, and you want to know who's crazy. Man, if you weren't crazy, you would be back across the Rio Grande sittin' in a nice, cool bar with your feet up. But I like crazies,' he chuckled. 'If I didn't, I wouldn't be here.'

Harding stared at the youthful face for a moment

or two in silence before nodding to Brennan.

'Get back to your position. And check on Haley on your way, think he may have been clipped.'

Without another word, Brennan rose in a half crouch and went off through the marsh, leaping from mossy stone to mossy stone, yellow buckskins reflecting in the dark, murky water.

The sun was low now, slanting obliquely across the trail where the bodies of men and horses lay sprawled in twisted figures of death. Flies buzzed and droned around the fallen. There were birds enough to be seen now. Buzzards. They were coming from everywhere, sensing their next feast, but they stayed aloft to wait in safety.

Little Mann said, 'I didn't make you upset, did I, Harding?'

'Don't worry, kid, he's a difficult man to insult or upset,' Brazos Bill called, and Harding realized that he was in earshot. 'A man has to be that when he is crazy. Ain't that so, Harding?'

Harding headed for Brazos' rock nest. He found the man comfortably lying on one side with a fragrant cigar stuck between his yellowed teeth.

Cotton Harding quickly dropped to one knee.

'What I said to the kid – Buck – goes for you too, Bill. No takin' fool chances with this lot. Now that we can see what we are up against, we will need every man we have.'

'Maybe not. They have stopped, if you hadn't noticed.'

Harding turned to look and saw that The Scourge

had drawn up along The Nape, just beyond rifle range. Sunlight glinted from guns, ammunition belts, bridles and metal fittings. Horsemen were packed solid from the banks of one lake to the banks of the other. Harding had half expected them to come pouring across in a flood after the first clash, but it seemed Juan Manuel Benitez was more cautious than he had counted on.

Cotton Harding lowered himself to a mossy rock and set his rifle aside. He nodded to Long-haired Jack, watching from his position fifty or so yards away, and to Tiger Sam and Bullock farther back. The men waved in response. They were all right.

'You were sayin', Harding?'

'I'm getting a bit tired of your gum-flapping, Bill.'

A shrug was the reply.

'It was Buck who claimed you were crazy first, not me.'

'You picked up on it mighty fast.'

Brazos Bill almost snorted. 'Only on account of it is the truth.'

Harding had a puzzled look on his face. 'How do you figure?'

Brazos Bill stretched out to an even more comfortable length and said lazily, 'Oh, I'm not travellin' down that kid's track. I mean about you robbin' folks to hire us and the such like. That ain't so crazy. No, what I see as crazy is the girl. . . .'

Harding's eyes narrowed with warning. 'Yeah?' he challenged.

'Yeah. When you told me about her first, I figured

113

you were lyin', Harding, coverin' up for something. But now that I know you are on the level about her, and you are doin' all of this for love, not because you wanted to hang Juan Manuel Benitez's scalp on your door handle as I hoped, or because you wanted to be some kind of big hero to a bunch of no-account Mexican villagers – I know we are in deep trouble.'

'Why is that?' Harding demanded.

'Because love and guns don't mix. You ought to know that. How many good gunfighters have you seen in your time that have been brought down in the end because they thought they had fallen in love? Hell, man, it is as fatal as slowin' down. The brain goes, and the reflexes ain't far behind. A man gets to thinkin' about fluff when he ought to be concentrating on stayin' alive.' Brazos Bill pantomimed playing a fiddle. 'Yessir, add love to gunfighting, and you wind up with slow music, flowers . . . lots of flowers, as in wreaths, and six feet of dirt on top of you.'

'I know what I am doin',' Harding snapped.

'So do I, Harding. I always know. And don't you forget that. You have bought my gun for a job of work, and I will do that job providin' you do yours. But if you start actin' crazy, like all people in love do sooner or later, then don't expect me to stick around and get my head shot off. I will be gone. Pfft! Just like that. I don't work for no crazy man.'

Harding raised himself to his haunches.

'You are still spendin' too much time worryin' about why I am doin' what I am, Brazos. I told you before, I will worry about that. You just keep your

114

damn head down and do what you do best – shoot. Leave me to do the thinkin'. Got it?'

'It is your money, so that must mean you are the boss, Harding.'

'That is so. And one last thing, Bill. Don't try running out on me. Every man I lose is goin' to increase the risk of my girl not comin' through this alive. You try and run on me, and I will have to kill you.'

Brazos Bill's laugh was forced.

'Now I am sure you are crazy, Harding. I am faster than you ever knew how to be.'

'Let's hope we don't have to find out for sure,' Harding murmured, and then he was on his way back to his post.

There was no smile on Brazos Bill's face as he took his cigar from his mouth and muttered, 'You sure are a fool, Harding. You ought to know there is no such thing as loving a gunfighter.'

Brazos Bill tried to convey contempt, but it came out sounding more like envy. He had never done anything for love in all his life.

It was just on dusk when Nina Marie Romero opened her eyes for the first time in nearly a week. The nurse ran for Doctor Hector Colón and found him on the stoop where he sat with the boy at his side, staring south. Most everyone in Hermanas Pozos had spent at least part of that late afternoon staring in the direction of that sound like summer thunder.

Doc Colón hurried inside to find his patient still

staring up at the ceiling. He took her by the wrist and consulted his pocket watch to take her pulse.

Then Nina Marie Romero astonished him by speaking.

'Who's there? That you, Cotton?'

'Señor Harding will be here in a moment, *señorita*,' Hector Colón lied. 'How are you feeling?'

But although Nina Marie Romero could whisper, she could not hear his voice. 'I was dreaming, dear . . .' she said. 'I was dreaming I heard guns in the distance. . . .'

Doc Colón stared across the bed at the face of his plump nurse. It seemed ironic that the first thing the patient should have heard since lapsing into the fierce grip of the fever had to be the awful sound of gunfire.

'Thunder,' he corrected. 'I will give you something to drink.'

'Guns,' Nina Marie Romero murmured, and her eyes closed again.

'Her pulse is still too rapid,' he said.

'But she must be getting better, *sí*?'

Doc Colón had to admit it. In truth, he saw great improvement in his patient and suspected that the fever could break at any moment. But walking from the room, the old man had mixed feelings. Of course he wanted her to survive, but on the other hand he didn't want her to pull through only to confront the horror which was coming . . . which Doc Colón knew must come.

'Eugenio returned while you are inside, Doctor,'

the boy told him, and pointed towards the cantina.

'Then I must find out what he has seen,' Doc Colón replied. 'While I am gone. . . .'

'*Sí*, I know. Water the roof.'

'You are a good boy.'

Doc Colón found Eugenio on the cantina porch surrounded by men from the town. Everyone was trying to talk at once, but because the mayor was louder than anyone else, his voice was heard.

'Did you see, Eugenio?' he called. 'Did you *really* see?'

Eugenio found the doctor's face with his bright eyes as he nodded. He was dust-stained and streaked in sweat. Eugenio alone, of all the citizens of Hermanas Pozos, had found the courage to ride out towards The Nape to observe what was taking place. He had been lucky, as his listeners realized when he told them what he had seen with his own eyes.

A fierce battle.

And too much death.

And a lot of bravery.

'But for Señor Harding and his *hombres*, Juan Manuel Benitez would be here on our doorstep at this moment,' he concluded. 'And let me tell you, The Scourge are very many. More than there ever were before. An army!'

'The *gringos*, Eugenio,' said Doc Colón. 'Were any slain?'

Eugenio shook his head.

'They fight with great courage but also with great skill, I think. Of course, Señor Harding was in the

117

very heart of the battle. He is a man of much bravery.'

'Well,' Colón murmured, gazing around, 'then he would be very lonely here tonight. . . .'

The remark was a criticism of himself as much as the others in the village, but some took offence.

'It is easy to have courage when one is born with a gun in the hand,' protested the *cantina* owner. 'It is not so easy when you are a simple, honest man confronting murderers.'

'Señor Harding is a brave man,' Eugenio insisted, 'and he has already done us all a great service.'

'You speak foolishly, Eugenio,' the mayor disagreed. 'Señor Harding would not lift one finger for all of us or all our children. None of the *pistoleros* would. They hold us in contempt. Señor Harding fights for the woman, and his amigos fight for *dinero*.'

'Well, at least they fight...' Eugenio replied, his voice trailing away.

The voices fell silent, and the atmosphere grew heavy with things unsaid. No man met directly the eyes of another. Their town was teetering on the very brink of disaster, and while they drank tequila and assured one another that they had no hope against the enemy, ten men, far less a number than all the able-bodied men in Hermanas Pozos, had ridden out to The Nape and stopped The Scourge in their tracks.

The feeling of something akin to shame was in the air as Doc Colón made his slow way back to his hospital.

Suddenly he started, stopped and turned.

The 'thunder' had begun again.

It sounded like Antietam, Wes Haley said, or any number of other battles he was in during the War between the States. The ground-trembling pounding of hundreds of hoofs, the hoarse battle cries of men and the metallic clash of gunfire – a cascade of warlike sounds flowing along the narrow length of The Nape and magnified by the serene surface of the two lakes.

A full cavalry charge.

No probing by forward scouts this time, however. This was Juan Manuel Benitez in full cry, storming headlong towards the marsh, intent on smashing his way through with sheer power and force of numbers.

'¡El Azotar! ¡El Azotar! ¡El Azotar!'

The terrible cry that had sounded the terror knell for the citizens in La Tenajo and Santa Rosa washed over the marsh as a pale moon skidded behind building clouds. The sudden darkness throbbed with peril.

In that darkness, skilled hands readied fast guns and calm faces turned toward The Nape.

They were ready. Ten of the most dangerous men in Old Mexico stood ready to fight either for their fee or for a cause. Whatever their reasons, there would be no backing down, no compromise. Killing was called for, and killing was what they did best of all. So let The Scourge come charging down the funnel and find out what it was like to ride at full gallop into a storm of lead.

Harding waited until they were quite close before touching off the short that was the signal.

Every gun in the marsh opened up simultaneously, and the night was made hideous by the blood curdling screams of mortally wounded men as the terrible scythe of fire lashed the riders' ranks. Men and horses fell in a maelstrom of blood and guts as the moon suddenly flashed forth again to reveal all.

Horsemen were piling up on their dead comrades as Buck 'Little' Mann wielded his shotgun. The frantic shouts of Juan Manuel Benitez urging his men on were swallowed by Harding's thundering six-shooters as he darted ahead to get in close to the chaos and empty saddle after saddle with guns that seemed unable to miss.

Whether inspired by Cotton Harding's example or unwilling to allow him to grab the glory was unclear, but suddenly Brazos Bill had joined him. They stood side by side, killing everything that came around or over the ghastly pile of death at the end of The Nape, until there was no way through for anybody and the enemy was retreating back.

'We got 'em walkin' backwards!' shouted an excited Little Mann, leaping from his rock nest with his shotgun in one hand and a six-gun in the other. 'Let's keep 'em goin', boys!'

Ignoring Harding's shot to come back, Little Mann went legging it around the death heap with Brennan and Long-haired Jack close on his heels, all eager to follow up the advantage.

They ran right into heavy gunfire.

Juan Manuel Benitez had mustered his forces and organized a rearguard while his tattered main force retreated. Within moments, the surfaces of the lakes were shimmering in the hot, yellow lick of gun flashes as gunfighters and rearguard battled it out. The gunmen had the skill, but The Scourge had the greater numbers. Avery Brennan was shot dead and Long-haired Jack Olinger was wounded. Buck 'Little' Mann dragged Long-haired Jack back to safety while Harding and Brazos Bill covered their retreat to the marsh.

By that time, Wes Haley and Otto Larsen had moved up to support Harding and Brazos Bill. Encouraged by the retreat from The Nape, a squad of bandit rearguarders made their way around the file of dead men on foot, intent on following up on their advantage. It didn't work. Harding, Brazos Bill, Haley and Larsen cut loose from both sides of the built-up section of the trail. The Mexicans fought back for a minute or so until they began losing men, and then backed off to their horses and ran for it.

The defence had held . . . for now.

They had lost Avery Brennan, but later when Harding sent Tiger Sam Sperry out on to The Nape to collect Brennan's body, he counted at a minimum of twenty-five dead Mexicans.

'Twenty-five *El Azotar* for one of us,' commented Brazos Bill, reaching for the makings of a cigarette. 'I guess that is something close to a fair trade.'

Nobody acknowledged his statement.

They were really earning their money.

With his yellow shirt glowing in the moonlight and his bright red scarf fluttering in the night wind coming off the lakes, Juan Manuel Benitez paced around and around the horse that carried the grinning skull of his dead son on the saddlehorn.

'*Pistoleros*!' he growled. 'Do you hear this, Marco? We ride to avenge you, and our way is blocked by *gringo pistoleros*.' He spat a sloppy mixture of saliva and tobacco. 'Mercenary scum!' Then he looked painfully confused. 'But who pays these butchers? If Hermanas Pozos were sold on the open market, it would not fetch enough to hire one of those *gringos* for a week. This is such a mystery that I do not comprehend. Who pays them? And why?'

Juan Manuel Benitez recommenced his pacing, and his lieutenants continued to stand in a silent circle, waiting for him to come down off the mountain of his rage and give fresh orders.

In other sections of the outlaw camp, wounds were being attended to and horses put out of their misery. One bandit, suffering from a shattered leg, gagged on the bullet he was biting as the limb was carelessly straightened and set.

Eventually, Juan Manuel Benitez cooled off and turned to the sharp-faced Erasmo. A cold-blooded killing mechanism, Erasmo could always be relied on to bring cold reason to such matters – as indeed he did now when called upon by his leader for advice.

'Talk to them,' he said simply.

Juan Manuel Benitez looked aghast.

'Talk with the filthy mercenaries while the fresh blood of the heroes they have slain is still dribbling into the lakes? Never!'

But Erasmo Gonzalez could be persuasive when necessary. He pointed out that despite the unsatisfactory outcome of the battle at the marsh, they must keep the fact in mind that the *pistoleros* were still not their enemy. It was Hermanas Pozos The Scourge wanted – and Erasmo was astute enough to add that Marco wanted it too. Erasmo's plan was to send in a good man under a flag of truce and find out what the *gringo*s would accept to withdraw.

'You are suggesting we pay them?' Juan Manuel Benitez gasped.

'They are, as you say, mercenaries. They are governed by money, nothing else. And we have such great wealth from our raids. . . .' Erasmo shrugged. 'Of course it offends me to deal with such scum, but we must not lose sight of our goal, great Benitz. Hermanas Pozos. . . .'

Hermanas Pozos.

The bandit king Juan Manuel Benitez had made the town the focal point of his fight back to outlaw eminence. He genuinely believed that only when he had erased Hermanas Pozos from the landscape would his honour be restored.

Erasmo Gonzalez was right. He did want Hermanas Pozos more than he wanted the heads of the *gringo* gunfighters.

CHAPTER 12

KILL OFTEN,
KILL QUICK

The gunfighters Bo Fisher and Otto Larsen squatted on their heels, going over the battle as it was still fresh in their minds, while fellow gunslingers, Wes Haley and Long-haired Jack Olinger, stood watch on The Nape about a hundred yards away.

Brazos Bill cleaned his guns, and Buck 'Little' Mann was repairing some small damage done to his beloved shotgun.

Cotton Harding had sent Tiger Sam Sperry and Tom Bullock behind Round Top to put Avery Brennan in the ground. In the meantime, he broke out provisions from the makeshift chuck wagon, which he now toted back towards the trail.

His cigarette had gone dead in his lips, and

Harding flicked the butt away, conscious of a tiredness in his muscles and especially his mind. Larsen and Fisher motioned him to join them after he distributed the grub. He went over, noting the bloodstains on a rock where Jack's leg wound had been patched up by Sperry. Larsen and Fisher had brewed coffee to go with the food. Harding lowered himself to a rock beside the two men and accepted a tin cup gracefully.

'Head up, Harding,' Bo Fisher counselled. 'We have done well, thus far.'

'You say so.'

Harding was not even thinking about the battle that was over, or of the battles to come yet. Nina Marie Romero filled his thoughts. He wanted to see her dearly.

Harding stared down at the white-handled guns riding his hips. At least for once they were doing a worthwhile job, he mused. They were holding back those bloody-handed bastards from Hermanas Pozos and the woman he loved.

The woman he loved. . . .

The phrase occupied his mind. Sure, he loved her. And she loved him back. But there was a big question nagging at the corners of his mind as he sat there drinking coffee and sniffing gun smoke. Could it work between the two of them? He wasn't shy of self-esteem, but neither was he blind to his flaws. He was a killer, of that there was little doubt. You could call it all kinds of things, but the profession he followed and had come to near master was that of killing.

125

Surely, a gentle young woman like Nina Marie Romero deserved something better than a killer for a husband?

Ex-killer, the back of his mind rationalized. Well, that might be so, Harding brooded, but a man's past had a way of coming back to haunt him. If they didn't know now in Kettle Springs, New Mexico, that Nina Marie Romero's man was a hired gun, a well-travelled killer, and overall a dangerous man, they would in time.

He realized that his companions were staring at him, that somebody had spoken his name several times.

'Huh?' he grunted. 'What did you say?'

Otto Larsen grinned.

'You were miles away, Harding. We was just sayin' as how Juan Manuel Benitez might decide he has had enough after the maulin' we handed him. What do you figure?'

'Your guess is as good as mine or any,' Harding replied. 'That charge sure cost him, and I don't reckon he would be dumb enough to pull that again. But he could have something else up his sleeve. He didn't get an army this big by being dumb.'

The words were barely out of his mouth when Wes Haley came down off The Nape to tell them a solitary Mexican was coming along the trail. The Mexican was under a white flag of truce. The Juan Manuel Benitez envoy had a surprise; he was prepared to buy them off.

'You have got to be joking,' Brazos Bill said, eyeing

the Mexican up and down with a smirk on his face. 'Nobody buys nobody off when they outnumber them twenty to one.'

The envoy insisted that he was sincere, and he produced a handful of jewels as proof.

The gunfighters passed the jewellery from hand to hand as Harding stated their position.

'You can tell Juan Manuel Benitez we are not quittin' for money or any other reason. We are here to defend Hermanas Pozos, and we are goin' to go on doin' it. Tell him that. . . .'

'Hey, just a blue-eyed minute,' Brazos Bill broke in. 'How long?'

'What? What are you talking about?' Harding scowled.

'I said, "how long",' Brazos Bill repeated, glancing at the others. 'I mean, when you signed us up, Harding, you told us you had a mighty risky job of work for us, but the pay was good. Now, this job ain't different from any other insofar as there has got to be some kind of time limit. Otherwise, we could be workin' forever. And it seems to me that for a job like this, which ain't so much a gunfight as a damn, full-scale war, that time limit for what we are bein' paid for ought to be pretty short.'

'Sounds right to me, I agree,' Bo Fisher said, his ancient grey whiskers stirring in the wind. 'I would not like you to think that we are goin' to set here forever tradin' lead with this Scourge bunch until they rub us all out, Harding.'

'We can talk about this later,' Harding snapped.

'Why not now?' Brazos Bill pressed. 'Hell, look at it this way, boys. We could clean up double here. Earn our money from Harding and then turn around and let old Juan Manuel Benitez buy us off so he can go through.'

'Nobody goes through,' Harding said quietly. 'Nobody gets through to Hermanas Pozos, now or later. Understood?'

'That sounds like you figure you have got us signed up for life,' Brazos Bill observed.

'Not for life,' Harding said, 'until the job is done. And it ain't done yet.' He turned to the Mexican and said, 'Go tell Juan Manuel Benitez I said he is a mule-diddlin' son of a whore. Tell him we ain't for sale, and that he needn't bother sendin' any more envoys in 'cause we will gun them down on sight. Tell him that if he keeps pushing, he will end up thinkin' that what happened to his mongrel son was plain good luck alongside what will happen to him. Have you got all of that, scum?'

The Mexican envoy jumped on his horse and rode around the death pile at a desperate gallop.

Staring from face to face, Cotton Harding saw men who wanted to say more about the situation, but were quickly silenced by the angry look across his face.

He did not give a damn.

'Get back to your places,' he angrily ordered.

He deliberately swung to face Brazos Bill and rested both hands on his gun butts. 'And if there is any more talk about sellin' out, I will put an end to it very quickly and once and for all.'

Even Otto Larsen and Little Mann began to back away.

There was a silence no man was willing to break, and then Brazos Bill started to grin.

'You are comin' apart, Harding,' he said gently. 'Never thought I would see the day.'

He held up his hands as Harding started to answer.

'OK, OK, we are getting back to our posts,' he said, and as he walked off Cotton Harding heard him shout, 'C'mon, you filthy greasers, you will never get a better chance than in the dark. But you will still find us here waitin' for you, 'cause we just discovered we are signed up for life!'

They were right, Harding thought as the last dim figure vanished in the gloom. There had to be a limit to how long they could be expected to stand off such huge odds. But the length of their commitment could only be determined by Nina Marie Romero and the fever that gripped her. He would leave Hermanas Pozos and The Nape only when they could take her back to their tiny village, not one blasted second before.

And while he stayed, *they* would stay.

Harding walked the rocky edge of the marsh with the night breeze in his teeth. Darker clouds were rolling across the sky and kept coming in from the north until all trace of moon glow had left the night sky.

The whole world he knew and could see was turning darker by the hour.

'What was that?' Wes Haley whispered.

'What was what?' Long-haired Jack Olinger replied.

A powerful, dark silhouette in the deep pre-dawn darkness, Wes Haley stood on The Nape trail, staring towards Lake Griego.

'I thought I heard something, Jack,' he added.

'What? Ducks?'

'What?'

'These lakes are full of ducks. And ducks wake up ahead of everything else on account of they are greedy and can't wait to start in feedin'. . . .'

Long-haired Jack stared back at Haley. 'How come you know so much about ducks, Wes?'

'I eat them every chance I get,' Haley fired back with a slight grin and quick pat of his stomach.

'Are you trying to be funny?'

Nerves were drawing a little taut. It had been a long day and seemingly longer night, and there was the stench of death that hung in the air.

'It ain't jittery to say you heard somethin' when you heard somethin',' Wes Haley said a little too aggressively. 'I reckon there is somethin' out there.'

'And I say there is nothing out there but stupid ducks,' snapped Jack.

But for once, Long-haired Jack the gambler-gunman was incorrect. And the axiom that 'everyone's entitled to make mistakes' didn't apply to men of their kind.

The sound Haley had heard was not ducks, but oars in the muffled oarlocks, propelling three fishing boats loaded with killers in big hats.

The outcome could have been devastating for Harding's men if Haley had not insisted on following up on his suspicions.

His warning bellow alerted the gunmen while his roaring rifle left the invaders in no doubt that they had been sighted.

A furious volley of gunfire came back from the boats, and as Long-haired Jack came limping down off the trail, Wes Haley, who had survived four years of war and nearly ten years of hiring out his guns, stopped the one that mattered most. He fell dead on the blood-splattered pebbles as the first Mexican waded ashore.

Jack drove the invader backwards with three bullets in the chest. He shot another man out of his boat and then backed away as the return fire heated up and the enemy came surging from the rocking rowboats.

Tom Bullock loomed out of the darkness to back Long-haired Jack as he stumbled to solid ground, favouring his injured leg. As Bullock opened up, more figures came running; Harding, Brazos Bill, Little Mann and Bo Fisher. Harding bellowed orders above the roaring guns, and Otto Larsen raced around to one side of the landing site to catch The Scourge in a crossfire. Bullock took up a position on the opposite side.

It was The Scourge leader's decision to rush

Bullock's position, which was closest to the trail. The action cost the Mexicans several men as Harding and Brazos Bill combined to pour in fire from their flank, but when Bullock was cut down by six-guns and rifles, the Mexicans poured towards the trail.

The American *gringos* went after them.

In the fierce, close-quarter struggle that followed, The Scourge's greatest liability proved to be their grimy off-white clothing. It made them far easier to see in the dark.

One by one, the Mexicans were hunted down and killed. The Americans were remorseless in their work. Harding shot a man through the head, then whirled and pumped four bullets into a giant who looked as big as a house as he charged headlong. As the big man fell at his feet, Harding was forced to drop flat under a sweep of rifle fire that was followed up by the roar of a shotgun. Little Mann's shotgun. Wounded Mexicans came reeling towards Harding under the driving impact of the shot in their backs. Harding picked them off systematically, and suddenly the lithe figure of Brazos Bill was there beside him, cleaning up what was left with the blazing Colts.

It was over by the time the sun came up, orange and angry over the twin lakes. Its light revealed a grisly scatter of bodies leading from the shoreline where the empty boats bobbed aimlessly, up to and across The Nape trail into the marsh where the seven Mexicans had made a final stand, and lost.

Among the seven dead was the body of Tom Bullock. Later, as he made preparations to ride into

Hermanas Pozos, Harding heard Brazos Bill say, 'Ten little gunfighters on their way to heaven – three got wiped out and then were seven.'

Harding said he had to see if Nina Marie Romero was well enough to travel before they were wiped out. Nobody tried to stop him. With the exception of a couple, Otto Larsen and Tiger Sam Sperry, who both loved to kill, the victorious *gringo* gunslingers felt they had seen about enough of Juan Manuel Benitez's Scourge army.

CHAPTER 13

SOME HOPE
AT LAST

For the very first time since her fever had consumed
her, Nina Marie Romero looked at Cotton Harding
with recognition, and she smiled. It was a wan, weak
smile, but a smile nevertheless.

'Sweetie,' she whispered, 'where have you been?'

Harding looked across the bed at Doc Colón, who
shook his head; he hadn't told her.

'Gettin' ready for our trip home, darling,'
Harding told her.

Again, Doctor Hector Colón shook his head, and
when the two men were alone, he gave it to Harding
simply and directly; Nina Marie Romero was vastly
improved, but she was not quite ready to travel.
Almost, but she was not strong enough at this time.

Harding was still on the porch, talking with the

medico as Eugenio arrived from the *cantina*. Unlike Doc Colón, Eugenio was very curious to know what all the shooting had been about overnight. Leaning against the wall rolling a cigarette, Harding brought him up to date, embellishing nothing, minimizing nothing. Harding told a story of slaughter, and that was the true story.

'How badly Juan Manuel Benitez wishes to kill us all,' Eugenio said somberly.

'Yeah,' Harding grunted in response.

'It is sad that you have lost three of your amigos, Señor Harding,' the boy said.

Harding shrugged with indifference. 'They knew what they were signing up for.'

Eugenio and Doc Colón studied the gunfighter. The bandanna around his throat was darkened by smoke, and there was a spatter of dried blood over his right boot and trouser leg. His eyes were tired and distant. Just looking at Harding made it possible to imagine the carnage that had taken place just outside of their town overnight.

Finally Eugenio spoke, 'Is it possible for you to continue your stand, Señor Harding?'

'What choice do I have, Eugenio? I don't see that I have another choice,' Harding replied with resignation.

'You realize we are in your debt, of course, *señor*?' The young man was trying to help the situation.

'I am not doin' it for any of you,' Harding snapped a little too harshly.

There had been too much blood for courtesies.

He got to his feet and was moving down the steps when he found himself confronted by a small child who offered him a red flower. Slowly, Harding's hard scowl faded. The little girl was no more than three years of age, he figured, barefoot and grimy but with enormous Spanish eyes and a rosebud mouth. Lifting his gaze, Harding saw two women standing at the far end of the building, watching and smiling sympathetically.

'The flower is for you, *señor*,' one of the woman called out.

'I don't need any damn flowers—' Harding began, but the child interrupted.

'For your *amigos*, *señor*.' She had a sweet voice.

Slowly, Harding lowered himself to his haunches and stared at the child at eye level. It seemed in that moment that despite all his time spent in Hermanas Pozos, this was the first resident he had really seen. Until that moment, they had all been just shapes and shadows to him, background to what was happening with him and Nina Marie Romero. But the little girl was real. She was a child who might grow up to be a lovely woman – if she grew up at all. If she wasn't killed before her next birthday.

'*Gracias*,' he said and stuck the flower through a buttonhole in his denim shirt.

Don José Antonio Parra was so wealthy and so highly respected that nobody summoned him anywhere. But that particular morning found the wealthy landowner closing in on the south side of The Nape in the company of Jorge Morales, who had been dispatched by the outlaw leader Juan Manuel Benitez to fetch him.

Don José, of course, could have ignored the summons, but Jorge had delivered Juan Manuel Benitez's message exactly as it had been given to him: Juan Manuel Benitez wished to confer with 'his noble *amigo*' concerning certain difficulties he was experiencing at the Twin Lakes. Juan Manuel Benitez had suggested that if Don José found himself unable to make the visit, this might have an 'unfortunate effect upon their valued friendship'.

Don José Antonio Parra, of course, had picked up on the not so veiled threat. Their 'friendship' was based on wary cooperation. Don José was a very obvious target of The Scourge, but since San Cristóbal could prove to be a very tough nut to crack, it suited Juan Manuel Benitez to merely exact light tribute and occasional cooperation from José Antonio Parra.

That was how it had been, and Parra wished to keep it that way. Hence his arrival on the shores of Lake Griego.

Don José Antonio Parra was not surprised to learn that Juan Manuel Benitez wanted assistance. It was known that Don José possessed a large flat-bottomed barge which was sometimes used to transport cattle and other goods across the lakes. Thwarted in his attempts to cross The Nape by land and encouraged by the near success of a landing in row boats, Juan Manuel Benitez was planning something bigger.

137

Although not anxious to take a step that might identify him too closely with The Scourge, Don José Antonio Parra was a realist. He was also bound and determined to get at Cotton Harding. Before long, the rich landowner gave the answer Juan Manuel Benitez wanted, and that was why he had come.

Something was in the air. Harding could sense it as he prowled the back of the marsh beneath yet another cloud-covered night sky. He missed seeing the stars. He had been expecting trouble ever since his return from Hermanas Pozos, trouble from Juan Manuel Benitez and trouble from some of his own. Although without incident, the day had been a long, hot one filled with tension. Waiting for something to break was harder than meeting the trouble head on.

The night wind blew in bringing with it the stench of death to him as he stood on the lake shore, gazing into the gloom. Throughout the day, buzzards had circled hungrily overhead, their evil shadows flickering constantly across the marsh and the sunbaked Nape and twin lakes.

Satches of conversation came to him on the breeze. Cotton Harding sighed and turned towards the trail. Sooner or later, he would have to find out what his men were up to, so it might as well be now. There was no time like the present.

As he climbed onto the trail, the voices from the rock nest below ceased. Or had it been just a single voice? Harding asked himself. Brazos Bill's?

'Are you boys keeping sharp?' he called down with

a hard whisper.

'As sharp as razors,' Brazos Bill answered with something close to a sneer. 'Sharp enough to know we are bein' used, Harding.'

Cotton hooked his thumbs in his shell belt and climbed down over the rocks that ridged the trail. He picked his way across the marsh to the rocks where Brazos Bill sat. Bo Fisher and Otto Larsen were there too with him. They should have been at their own posts, but Harding decided not to make an issue of it. He sensed there were bigger things to be considered at the moment.

'Used?' he asked, resting one foot on a rock. 'How exactly is that?'

Brazos Bill stood up to face Cotton Harding.

'You know how, Harding. You hired us to stop Juan Manuel Benitez, but now you seem to expect us to keep on doin' it till doomsday. That wasn't the deal, *amigo*.'

'I did not know it would run like this,' Harding replied honestly. 'I figured Nina Marie would be well enough to travel before this. I didn't know Juan Manuel Benitez had so many men or that he would be so all-fired determined to take this town.'

'So, you can't blame us if we quit, can you?' Brazos Bill shot back.

'Quit?' The notion had not come to mind for Harding.

'Quit,' Brazos Bill repeated. 'That is, unless you come up with more money. I mean, we are greedy and we will admit to that. Feed us more dough for

139

the extra work, and you have got us. Ain't that so, pardners?'

'Bill does have a point and makes a certain amount of sense, Harding,' Fisher said.

'Does he now?' Harding asked as he focused on Brazos Bill.

Bo Fisher and Otto Larsen would sooner fight than do anything else, Harding knew, but Brazos Bill had convinced them that they were being short-changed or, as he had put it, 'used'.

'Well, there isn't any more money,' he continued, and then he added flatly, 'and you are not quitting.'

Brazos Bill let out a long, whistling breath.

'How is that again, Harding?' he asked with just a hint of menace. The tension mounted.

'I told you before,' Harding replied. 'I can't afford to lose any more men.'

'You can't afford to keep us either,' Brazos Bill sneered angrily.

'It is too late for anybody to back out now. . . .' Harding said as he absently fingered the faded flower in his buttonhole. 'If we pulled out, it would be like a dam busting open. Benitez would be in Hermanas Pozos in no time at all. These people would not stand a chance.'

'You said yourself your gal had picked up,' Brazos Bill snapped, shedding his mocking manner. 'So, take a chance, Harding. Load her up and get out of there.'

'It is not just Nina Marie. . . .' Harding said almost tearfully.

The three men stared back at him.

'Who the hell else is here?' demanded Brazos Bill.

Although he was surprised to hear himself admit it, Harding said, 'There is the town. That is who else – women, children, good people. . . .'

'There is something wrong with you,' Brazos Bill said with a shake of his head. 'Maybe you have had too much sun. But if you figure you can get us het up over a bunch of Mexican villagers. . . .'

A soft whistle interrupted. It came from Buck 'Little' Mann. As Brazos Bill fell silent, they heard the sound that had attracted Little Mann. The thud of hoof beats out along The Nape.

'Here they come!' Harding hissed. 'Otto, Bo, back to your positions.'

The men vanished immediately leaving Harding and Brazos Bill alone. Cotton Harding had his right hand on his six-gun.

'You are the best gun in the bunch, Brazos,' Harding admitted. 'If you went, we would likely all go down. That is why you are staying put.'

'And if I say go to hell?' Brazos Bill fired back.

'We fight. It is simple as that,' replied Harding directly.

'I am faster than you, Harding,' Brazos Bill said sternly.

'You would have to prove it.' Harding stood his ground.

'Hey!' Little Mann called softly. 'Are you jokers aimin' to jaw these Mexicans to death, or what?'

With a parting look of warning, Harding turned

141

his back and left the rock nest, conscious of Brazos Bill's eyes on him as he climbed up the trail.

He stared south towards a pile of the dead, and moments later, the crack of a rifle from the pile sent him diving for cover.

And so began a strange hit-and-run series of skirmishes that lasted several hours, with the Mexican invaders touching off potshots from The Nape, backing up when the gunfighters went after them and then returning to snipe again.

Otto Larsen took a wound early on, and much later a Scourge came in too close and was almost blown in half by Little Mann's big shotgun. Those incidents aside, Cotton Harding had the feeling all along that this tippy-tag gunfight didn't ring true, that if Juan Manuel Benitez had really intended giving them trouble he would have used a bigger stick than half a dozen men who seemed more interested in teasing than in actually fighting.

And then Tiger Sam Sperry was whistling down at them from his lookout on Round Top. The sound was immediately engulfed by a sudden roar of gunfire from somewhere beyond.

Harding was stunned. There was nobody beyond Round Top, just the expanse of the twin lakes.

Tiger Sam's big voice boomed down at them, 'Scourge, Harding. We are being hit from the flank!'

Tiger Sam's guns blasted as Harding, Little Mann and Long-haired Jack Olinger went streaking away from the marsh. In the gloom, they saw swift moving figures surging through their camp behind Round

Top, big-hatted figures, blasting as they came.

The three gunfighters opened up with a murderous volley, and were supported by Tiger Sam from above. Men fell on every side, howling and dying. Harding legged it through the battle scene as terrified horses broke and ran. Two Mexicans loomed up in front of him. He cut them down with two shots and kept running. He had to find out where the bandits were coming from.

Something bulky and dark was just visible on the water as he scrambled over the stones along the shore. Harding moved closer, guns at the ready. He was challenged in Spanish. He opened up with both .45s and the voice went silent. Then they returned fire. He realized then that the torn-up track where he lay had been made by horse hoofs. Many hoofs. The tracks led due north, away from the water.

Straight on towards Hermanas Pozos!

Suddenly, Cotton Harding was up and running back the way he had come with bullets zipping through the darkness all around him. Something close to panic was clawing at his brain.

He almost put a bullet into the bulky shape that materialized ahead of him before he recognized Tiger Sam Sperry.

'What the hell is goin' on, Harding?' Tiger Sam Sperry asked.

Harding ran right past Tiger Sam without a reply, making for the camp. Tiger Sam spun around and charged after him.

'What is the matter with you?' he panted. 'What

did you see back there?'

Harding cursed as he stumbled over a dead Mexican. As he got to his feet, Little Mann and Long-haired Jack appeared, leading horses that had broken away during the shooting.

'Get mounted!' Harding gasped, lunging for a brown stallion. 'We are heading for Hermanas Pozos.'

'What in tarnation for?' Tiger Sam demanded.

Once he was astride the horse, Cotton Harding forced himself to calm down.

'They came across the lakes in a cattle boat,' he said. 'I don't know how many, but plenty by the tracks. Only about a dozen came after us to keep us busy; all the rest of the bastards are headin' right for the town. Tiger Sam, go tell Brazos Bill and the others what happened here. I want you and Fisher to stay here and guard The Nape, and Brazos Bill and Otto to follow us to Hermanas Pozos.'

'But. . . .' Tiger Sam began, but Harding cut him off sharply.

'No "buts", mister!' He snapped harshly. 'Just do what I say!'

Then he was gone in the darkness, leaving Buck 'Little' Mann and Long-haired Jack Olinger to scramble astride their mounts and follow him as big Tiger Sam Sperry ran back to The Nape.

The moon had stayed hidden all night, but now the clouds had parted a bit, and the bloodied shore was bathed in silver light.

CHAPTER 14

THE MEASURE OF A MAN

A Mexican bandit came running from an adobe, clutching a carbine rifle as Cotton Harding entered Hermanas Pozos astride a lathered, foam-slobbering horse.

'Marco!' the Mexican bandit screamed at the top of his lungs. It was the last sound he would ever make. Harding's .45 thundered and the bullet opened his skull and tossed his brains back against the wall of the adobe.

Harding's horse did not miss a stride as it sailed over another corpse in its run for the town square.

Hermanas Pozos was filled with the crash of guns, and the air was thick with dust and gunsmoke as Harding covered the last breathless yards to the town square.

He dreaded to think what he might find and tried desperately to keep Nina Marie out of his mind. Then the square was behind him, and his eyes widened as he saw a pitched battle raging – almost directly in front of Doctor Hector Colón's.

He had to blink twice before he could believe what he was seeing.

The 'gutless' citizens in their shabby cotton clothes were locked in mortal combat with a swarm of *El Azotar* horsemen. The townspeople were using old guns, staves, pitchforks and other items as weapons, and some merely used rocks. There were bodies all over, and many of them were The Scourge. Even as Cotton Harding paused to reload his six-shooters, he saw Eugenio drag a raider from his horse and plunge a crimson blade into his throat.

With new hope, Harding was heeling forwards when the drumbeat of hoofs and a stutter of gunfire from a side street heralded the arrival of Little Mann and Long-haired Jack.

Harding went for the foe like a terrier clearing a barn of rats. The sheer, headlong ferocity of his attack seemed to be his safeguard as wild-eyed Mexican bandits turned to see him coming, and his twin white handles belched flame and delivered death.

The Mexican raiders were still reeling from this one-man hurricane when Little Mann and Long-haired Jack swept in from another angle, dealing death with every touch of their triggers.

The ragged cheer that rose from the villagers of

146

Hermanas Pozos grew stronger as The Scourge faltered and began to give ground.

Juan Manuel Benitez, leader of *El Azotar*, urged his men to fight on, and they surged after the enemy, leaving a score of dead from both sides in their wake.

As Cotton Harding approached the hospital, with a flaming pistol in each hand and a crippled *El Azotar* struggling to get out from under his horse, he darted a glance at the building and felt his heart skip one full beat.

Two pale faces staring from the window. Doctor Hector Colón and his love, Nina Marie.

Harding lowered his right-hand gun and shot the crippled raider through the back of the neck. A man shouted to him from a porch. A *Rurale*!

'Erasmo Gonzalez!' the *Rurale* shouted, indicating a lean rider cutting down a lane way. 'He is the leader, *gringo*!'

Harding went after his man. Erasmo had the better horse, but Harding rode with greater determination. And when the Mexican bandit was forced to slow down to round a corner, Harding drilled a bullet through his shoulder and knocked him clean out of his saddle. Erasmo fell hard and demolished a chicken coop on his way to the ground.

His gun smoked again as Harding's mounted figure towered above him.

Harding ducked the bullet and pounced on the man from the saddle. The struggle was over in seconds.

With the unconscious Erasmo slung over his

shoulder, Harding trotted back down the alley to the square and came face to face with the *Rurale*. The soldier was leaning on a stick, favouring a bloodied leg. He gestured across the square, where a dozen townsmen were swarming over three screaming Scourge, pounding them to death with staves.

Looking calmly as they reloaded their guns were Long-haired Jack Olinger, Buck 'Little' Mann, and Brazos Bill.

The battle of Hermanas Pozos was over.

Cotton Harding held Nina Marie's hands as he listened to the story of what had happened in Hermanas Pozos.

When The Scourge horsemen descended without warning, there was pure panic at first. When it was realized that the raiders were making directly for Doc Colón's, Eugenio opened up from the town's cantina and shot one of the horsemen down. Other horsemen returned his fire but Erasmo was still leading the main bunch directly to the hospital. Two bandits rushed inside to drag Nina Marie from her sickbed onto the porch.

That was where the 'miracle' of Hermanas Pozos had taken place, when the poor men and women of the town realized that the enemy had come for Harding's woman. After all, it was Harding who had been holding Benitez at bay for so long while they cowered in their 'safe' little town, drinking and praying.

Hermanas Pozos's dormant courage stirred,

growled and then came roaring to life as Eugenio ran from the cantina with his gun in his hand to attack the raiders alone. The young man would certainly have died, had not the mayor, of all people suddenly appeared in his doorway with his rifle. When he fired on The Scourge mob, it was like a signal to set the people aflame.

The *Rurale*, the gunfighters learned now, had arrived an hour before the raiders with news that nobody had anticipated. The *Rurales* were on the march against Juan Manuel Benitez at last and would reach the town within twenty-four hours. The officer had been sent ahead to bring the news and, if possible, to help Hermanas Pozos hold out against The Scourge.

Then it was Erasmo's turn to fill in the remaining blank spots. The wounded raider was reluctant to talk at first, but he changed his mind in a hurry when Little Mann forced his jaws apart and rammed the double barred muzzles of his shotgun up against the bandit's back teeth.

Then they could not stop him from talking.

It was José Antonio Parra who provided the cattle barge, and Parra who had first suggested to Benitez that the raiding party take Nina Marie hostage in order to force Harding's surrender. After that, they were to put the town to the torch and ride back to clear the marsh and enable the main force to cross The Nape.

'Twenty-four hours,' Harding murmured. 'They can't get here any quicker?'

149

The *Rurale* shook his head.

'We have been force-marching for many days, Señor Harding. We can do only so much.'

'How many scum have you got across The Nape?' Harding asked the bandit Erasmo.

Little Mann smacked the wounded Mexican across the head to loosen his tongue once again. Otto had been killed in the town fight and Little Mann was in no mood to be gentle.

'More than a hundred. . . .' Erasmo's face sagged. 'You *pistoleros* have killed so many of our brave men . . . but there are many more who will bury you.' He jerked his chin at Eugenio. 'And your filthy town, too.'

'Well, that is not our problem any longer, is it, Harding?' Brazos Bill drawled. 'I mean, it is plain as paint that your lady is all right to travel at last – which is all we have been waitin' for, isn't it?' He spread his hands as he spoke. 'The townspeople have found their nerve, Benitez is cut down by almost half, and the law is on the way. Why, it is almost like a happy ending. So let's whistle in Tiger Sam and Fisher and get goin'.'

Harding squeezed Nina Marie's hand. Doc Colón had told him that her fever had broken just after his last visit, and that she was now able to travel.

Even so, Cotton Harding could not see everything as the 'happy ending' described by Brazos Bill. Everything the man said was true enough, except for one thing. Despite the resistance thrown up by Eugenio and the townspeople, he knew that

Hermanas Pozos could not defend itself against the full, vengeful fury of Juan Manuel Benitez's *El Azotar* if they came pouring across The Nape during that vital twenty-four hours.

Neither Nina Marie nor his men could understand what was wrong when Harding walked out without a word. He had an overpowering feeling that he was searching for something or someone as he walked the battle-littered square, but he had no idea what it was until he found her.

It was on a back street, where urchins were robbing the corpse of a raider, that he saw her seated on a stoop with her mother, staring out wide eyed at a world she could not yet fully comprehend.

The child who had given him the flower.

When Harding and Nina Marie and the gun-slingers were gone, she would remain here. The citizens had nowhere else to go. They were filled with pride over the defeat of The Scourge, Harding knew, but they did not understand that with him and his gunfighters gone, they would still face annihilation.

The *Rurales* would arrive much too late to save Hermanas Pozos. They would march in to relieve a town that no longer existed. And the little girl would be one tiny corpse among the many.

Cotton Harding stopped in the middle of the street, and then he slowly turned back towards the square. He was smiling. It was always good to know what you had to do.

CHAPTER 15

A BEGINNING
AND AN END

The marriage between Cotton Harding and Nina Marie Romero took place in the tiny town church about an hour or so later. The bride alternately smiled and wept, so happy to be marrying the man she so dearly loved at last, but dismayed because he planned to send her ahead with Brazos Bill while he returned to The Nape to 'tie up a few loose threads'.

She tried to change his mind again after the ceremony, believing now that they were married she would hold more sway over him, but Harding insisted that she leave as they had planned. It was too dangerous for her to stay in Hermanas Pozos with The Scourge still a threat, he reasoned. There was no guarantee that the enemy might not try to seize her again either. She would be safe with Brazos Bill;

Harding would catch up with them as soon as he could.

'Always the big hero, huh, Harding?' Brazos Bill said as Harding prepared to leave for The Nape.

'How is that?' Harding replied, poker-faced.

'You don't fool me,' Brazos Bill sneered. 'I see through you like glass. You mean to go back to The Nape and try to hold off The Scourge until the *Rurales* come.'

Buck 'Little' Mann and Long-haired Jack Olinger blinked in surprise. Harding had told them he merely wanted them to return to The Nape with him to collect their gear and the friends who they had lost.

'That ain't the case, is it, Harding?' Little Mann asked with concern. 'I mean, with Otto Larsen dead and Brazos gone with Nina Marie and the rest of us worn thin and all shot up. . . .'

'I keep tellin' you not to listen to Brazos Bill,' Harding shrugged. 'The poor feller just can't help but run off at the mouth – so, are you two comin' with me or not?'

He started off without them, only to find his way blocked by Eugenio.

'*Amigo*,' he said quietly, 'is this the truth?'

'Let go of my horse, Eugenio,' Harding said directly.

'If you mean to fight more out there, we shall fight with you, Señor Harding,' the young man announced.

'No, you won't. What you have to do, Eugenio, is

153

fortify this town in case The Scourge do break through. Keeps spirits high. Make sure that every able-bodied man is carrying a weapon. We will take care of Benitez.'

Eugenio's face was grave and admiring.

'Then you *do* fight?' he whispered.

Cotton Harding did not reply, for Long-haired Jack and Little Mann were now at his side. He just threw a casual salute and started off across the square. He stopped only once, and that was to wave to Nina Marie – his wife – on Doc Colón's porch. He was thinking how long twenty-four hours could be.

The hours were beginning to feel like an eternity.

The first of The Scourge showed up at daybreak almost on cue. He came riding along The Nape at the walk, a lean-bodied *bandito* wearing crossed ammunition bandoleers with a heavy carbine slung over one shoulder. He rode to the limit of rifle range from the marsh, and then he halted and lifted his field glasses.

'That does it!' growled Bo Fisher. 'He is checkin' us out before they come across. Well, it has been fun, Harding, but the fun is over. *Adios.*'

Harding gusted cigarette smoke at the grizzled old gunslinger.

'Never, in a million years, thought I would see the day you would run out of guts, Bo,' Harding declared.

'You ain't gonna get me that way,' Bo Fisher growled as he swung on his horse. 'Maybe you can sucker some of these younger gunmen in like that, but this old shootist is too long in the tooth, Harding.' He looked at the others. 'Any of you fellers comin'? Or are you all tired of livin'? Like Harding here?'

The animal-like Tiger Sam Sperry looked sheep-ish.

'Reckon you will understand if I go along with the old goat, won't you, Harding? I mean, what you are fixin' to do here, without Otto or Brazos or. . . .'

'Sure, I understand, Tiger,' Harding said. 'I under-stand that I thought I was hirin' a man, but it turns out I could not tell a gunfighter from a gutless wonder.' He jerked his thumb. 'Go on, get lost! This marsh is gunfighter territory, boys. There is no place here for anybody with a yellow streak.'

It didn't work – Bo Fisher and Tiger Sam Sperry left anyway. Now Harding was down to just two men, Buck 'Little' Mann and Long-haired Jack Olinger. They thought he was crazy too, but their friendship was stronger, and they were prepared to stay.

'Well, well,' Little Mann grinned as the silence descended. 'Just the three of us now, against half of Mexico, huh? Sounds fair enough odds to me, don't you reckon, Jack?'

'If I saw those odds on a table,' replied the gunman gambler. 'I would bet my life on them. . . .'

Harding checked out his fob watch. Eighteen hours. He looked up. The Scourge scout was riding away at a lope.

There were still more than seventeen hours to go

when the three gunfighters saw the horde of horsemen start across The Nape. The Scourge came slowly, and there was murderous purpose in their slowness.

Juan Manuel Benitez was strangely calm.

Usually, the prospect of battle made him noisy and swaggering. Today he sat his saddle with dignity – head held high and eyes on the way ahead – almost like a true general. This was no wild, drunken raid. This was war. The enemy had mauled him again and again, but Benitez knew that today he would be victorious. Today.

His right hand stroked the skull of his dead son.

'Smile, my boy . . . show me the good omen.'

To Juan Manuel Benitez's eyes at least, the naked skull did seem to smile.

Benitez lifted his heavy arm, held it high for a long moment and then brought it forward.

One hundred and twenty men surged down The Nape.

Three guns welcomed them but not kindly.

Long-haired Jack Olinger was dying, but he was not dead just yet and was still able to shoot.

'One more!' he panted as he worked his triggers to drive yet another howling Scourge out of their saddle. His hand trembled as he took aim again, but he steadied at the vital moment and triggered once more. A running figure hit the ground.

Then Long-haired Jack slumped over like someone who was very, very tired. Harding came lunging up with six-guns yammering to drive back the human wave attempting to engulf them.

Harding snatched the cigarette from between his teeth and placed it in Jack's mouth.

'Much obliged, Harding,' the man murmured.

He took one draw and died.

Minutes later, Cotton Harding and Buck 'Little' Mann were driven back to the rock nest which Brazos Bill had set up, seemingly an eternity before all of this.

They did not know how long they had been fighting now; there was no time to stop or think, only time enough to fight. To burn powder, to kill, to hold back the tide.

To fight for their lives.

The death pile was twice the size it had been before, but still the Mexican raiders came. Urged on by their bandit king – Juan Manuel Benitez's booming voice, the bandits came in wave after wave. Harding and Little Mann mowed them down as swiftly as they could reload and fire – until the bullet with Buck 'Little' Mann's name on it came whistling through the smoke-filled air.

Then Cotton Harding was alone with two hot six-guns, a deep wound in his side and his face set towards the foe.

He fired and a man howled in agony. A huge figure loomed atop the death pile, clutching a human skull. Harding tried to get a bead on him, but the gunfire sent him ducking for cover. He lay panting and bleeding, knowing they would come now, knowing he had failed.

They would ride over him – and then over Hermanas Pozos.

Harding started as a gun yammered within inches of his head. It was Brazos Bill, pouring a two-gun fire at the enemy and forcing them back yet again.

'Don't take this wrong, Harding,' Brazos Bill drawled as he dropped behind the boulders to reload. 'We ain't friends, and I still think you are a damn fool. And don't you worry about your pretty woman, neither. I sent Bo and Tiger Sam on with her when I decided to come back. She is happy enough. Still thinks she will meet up with you. But you and me know better than that, don't we, Harding?'

Harding got up on one knee and killed two men with two bullets. Benitez's incessant voice boomed out, urging his warriors on.

'You are full of surprises, Brazos,' he said softly.

'Ain't I though? You ready to get that sumbitch Benitez?' the gunslinger asked.

'What?' was all Harding could say in response.

'I watched this ruckus for half an hour before Little Mann got hit. I can see how this shin-dig is goin'. These bastards are tired of fightin' and dyin', but Benitez keeps pushin' them on. He will go on doin' that until we are finished, and then he will do it again in Hermanas Pozos. He will do it soon, too, Harding. That means you will die for nothin', because the town will go – just like Benitez planned all along. But if he is dead, do you reckon these Mexicans that are bein' pushed as hard as they are

158

are goin' to worry about the townspeople? Hell no. They ain't crazy. It is only Benitez that is *loco*, and we are about to cure him of that. Keyrect?'

Cotton Harding stared in Brazos Bill's eyes, and something unsaid passed between them.

Harding smiled as he pumped his Colt .45s full of fresh shells.

'We sure the hell are . . . *amigo*.'

Brazos Bill extended his right hand, and Harding took it in quick, firm grip.

Then they stood up together and charged behind four bucking, flaming guns.

It was totally unexpected. It was, in fact, insane. The Scourge stumbled back.

A huge voice roared, 'Destroy them! Why do you delay, *amigos*?'

It was a combination of shock and the furious fire-power that threw the enemy swarm off-balance, and now the two fast-moving figures came within six-gun range of the death pile, and they were shooting at just one man.

Juan Manuel Benitez died in a storm of bullets. His great carcass came spinning down over the rotting corpses. The skull fell from his dead hands and shattered as Harding and Brazos Bill turned to fight their way back – the impossible way back.

The enemy guns smoked, and the morning was filled with the roar of battle as the two gunfighters moved towards the marsh – swiftly at first, then slower and slower as the brutal bullets took their toll on them.

The sun seemed uncommonly bright as it shimmered across the twin blue lakes. Harding's guns blazed but their roar seemed far away. He smiled. He remembered that it was his wedding day.

'Have a good life, Mrs Harding,' he breathed as Brazos Bill went down.

His guns blazed again as the dark horde closed in. Into the darkness with him he took the sure knowledge of what it was to be a man.